DAVE NEEDS TO STAY DEAD

C. C. YORK

ISBN: 979-8-218-37655-0

This is a work of fiction. Any resemblance to actual events or persons, living or dead, is entirely coincidental.

EDITOR: AMY CARDEN
COVER DESIGNER: MARY ANN SMITH

1

Coffee & Murderers

THE PROBLEM WITH MURDERING your husband is the paranoia that follows.

Maria Fever wrapped her oversized cardigan around her as she squeezed behind the barista counter, nodding once to her boss, Cate, and ignoring Dave's wide face on the television behind her head. She made minimal eye contact with the line of customers lingering on the other side. Mama Cate's was the town's only coffee shop/wine bar/bookstore/post office, so it wasn't unusual to have a crowd once the early October winds picked up. But the morning still felt off. *It's just the murder-paranoia*, she told herself, unconvincingly, as she picked up the bag of coffee beans to grind.

"I can't believe Shane Bolles is coming back," Shirley said over the dregs of a cappuccino. "If I made it out of Hinnewatcha, I'd never come home." The town's deputy often started her conversations with how much she hated this town. Her next favorite topic was how much she hated her job. "Anyhoo, Cate, I'll be seeing you. I'm off to report to Satan. Maria, nice seeing you out and about again."

Maria breathed in through her nose like the meditation podcasts taught her, dropped her shoulders, and let the old bag's comments roll over her. Levi Madison, Hinnewatcha's police chief and Shirley's boss, was a bit cold to most, but Maria became his biggest fan the day he stood over Dave's stiff body and declared it to be an accidental overdose. *He's just shy*, she thought, and the recurring daydream of him noticing her outside of her late husband's demise began to play while she doled out coffee and pastries to the regulars.

She appreciated the routine of a coffee shop and the rustle of turning pages. But every bark of laughter or scrape of a chair made Maria want to jump out of her skin. *It's your first day back. Give it time,* she told herself. She had only been in Hinnewatcha for a couple years, but most regulars knew her and that she'd just lost her husband. She forced her lips to curve up into a polite smile and thanked anyone that offered her their condolences, all while keeping an eye on the clock that never moved. Maria released her death grip on the frothing pitcher to help Cate bring in the heavier Amazon boxes.

"I'm gonna open this one," Cate announced as they heaved the first one on the counter.

"Can't, Cate. It's illegal to open someone else's package," Maria said, smiling to herself at Cate's perpetual need to snoop.

"Yeah, but what on earth could Mrs. Wilson need with a box this big? What if it's a bomb? Haven't you heard? Democrats are sending bombs to the elderly."

"That's a new one," Maria said, blowing back an errant curl that slipped out of her clip. "We're low on pumpkin spice, do you want me to make more tonight?"

Dave's face flashed again as the story ran another loop. *Dumpy bastard.* She smiled once more, growing ever more pleased with herself for choosing a photo he always hated.

Cate didn't answer, and Maria realized her mistake when she looked back from the TV to see Mrs. Wilson's box only halfway opened. Cate leaned over the box, gesturing at her with the box cutter. "You sure you're ok, Maria? I appreciate you coming back in and all, but it hasn't been that long since Dave… you know, died."

"Smooth, Catey," Cate's husband drawled from behind his paper. The worn-in green recliner would have a perfect indention of Hamby's derriere when he stood up, and he'd likely carry on multiple conversations without ever looking up from the newspaper in hand.

Maria ignored Hamby and dropped her smile, reminding herself that she's supposed to be struggling with grief. The lie slipped off without trouble. "It's better when I'm busy, Cate. Sitting at home, waiting on Isabelle to get home from school is too much. The house is too quiet unless I'm moving."

"OK," Cate said, nodding once. "Then, yes. Bring in more pumpkin spice. I can't believe we're barely into October and those bloodsucking Millennials are already killing our pumpkin spice reserves. I swear to Fall Jesus that if I see another felt hat, I'll lose it."

Hamby actually set down his paper. The lines around his eyes wrinkled even more around his mischievous smile.

"They're trying to expand the entrance to Firefly Farms this year so more traffic can flow in for photo sessions."

Maria's grief status fell by the wayside when Cate launched into her diatribe about selfies and the general ruination of society by the younger generations. Hamby winked once at Maria as he snapped his paper back open.

Her gratitude for this job rose even higher.

***

Maria took another sip of her tea, trying to ignore the urge to look at whoever was watching her this time. Every whisper or side glance convinced her that at any moment someone would call her out for what she was. *Murderer.* She resumed shading the pumpkin on the chalkboard in front of her while her eyes skimmed the sidewalk. A trio of women stopped nearby, boots to thighs and clad in scarves, to take a photo under one of the older elms, not noticing her. Hinnewatcha was quintessential New England, the postcard of fall and Christmas cute. Tourists would come in droves for the next three months, bolstering the businesses that would otherwise wither in the gas-lamp lined town.

She smiled at the women's staged poses and thought back to the first time she came to Hinnewatcha. A similar giant, gnarled, orange and yellow elm made Maria stop here two years ago to begin with. She was a single mother, broke, and looking for a change from downtown Los Angeles, and Hinnewatcha was the antithesis of smog and lost boys racing to become bad men. A polite, yet pointed, cough came from behind her, and unease replaced the warmth of that memory. *Easy,* she thought before turning. *You are not hiding anything.*

The man-boy was gangly but tall enough that she assumed he worked for the nearby college paper. "Mrs. Fever?" He asked.

Maria stifled a groan, she had hoped the reporters would have moved on from Dave's death by now. She smiled, shielding her eyes from the bright autumn sun to look up at his face. "That's me. And you are?"

"Myles, Ma'am. I'm with the University of Vermont and I'm studying to be a journalist. Well, I am a journalist of sorts." Myles rambled—too fast and too long—occasionally slipping on his words before he got to the point. "Can you answer some questions for me?"

"I'm sorry, I can't answer anything while there's an ongoing investigation. Police orders." Maria dusted the chalk from her hands on her apron and began to gather the scattered pieces littering the sidewalk. She dropped two pieces, hands shaking. *Relax, Maria, you're not fleeing a scene. Just going about your job.* She balled a fist and her fingernails dug into her palm, steadying her for a moment.

"Right, but I don't want to know about the murder per se," Myles said as he stooped down to help Maria gather chalk. "I just want to know your thoughts about Shane Bolles picking up the case."

"You mean Levi? I mean, the Police Chief, Levi Madison?"

"No," Myles shook his head. "No one likes that guy. I'm talking about *the* Detective Bolles... from Bravo's *Dead Don't Lie?*" Myles did a little pantomime of what Maria assumed a character from Clue would do.

She shrugged. "I'm sorry? I don't know who that is, but

I would have been informed if Chief Madison was no longer working on my husband's case."

"You're about to freak out then. Detective Bolles is the world's best cold case detective. Out of five seasons, he's never left a case unresolved. And he decided to pick up Dave Fever's case because it came from his hometown."

A hundred thoughts scattered across Maria's mind, each one more urgent than the last. It took every ounce of willpower to plant her feet and not leave the budding reporter far behind. "That's great news," she said, swallowing the lump in her throat. "A little odd though, don't you think? A cold case detective decides to pick up a two-week old case that everyone knows was an accidental overdose?"

"Not everyone," Cate's booming voice pelted over Maria's shoulder, startling her and making her drop more chalk. "Most people 'round here think he was murdered on account of that no good brother of his. Definitely a drug deal gone bad."

"Not helpful, Cate," Maria said, but Myles latched on, bypassing Maria for her boss hovering in the doorway.

His thumb flew over the note app on his phone, "Greg Fever? He's been all over the news telling reporters that his brother was murdered, so what would make you think he did it?"

"Well I don't know anything, but—"

Maria ducked inside the shop as Cate began rattling off all the things she thought she knew. The things everyone thought they knew. *That's the problem in a small town. If this was LA, no one would have even noticed a guy like Dave had died,* Maria thought as she hung her dirty apron on a nail by the nonfiction bookshelf.

Hamby grunted a goodbye, nose still in his paper, as she slipped behind Cate still blathering to the rapt college reporter. She wrapped her tartan scarf around her and headed towards the elementary school, leaving behind a trail of scattered, browning leaves on the sidewalk. Maria paused at the pharmacy window a few storefronts over to rehang a paper bat that fell off in the wind, and nodded to the old couple from Drew Lane playing backgammon in the pocket-sized Applegate Park. A group of teens lounged nearby in the manicured grass, passing around their phones and laughing. Everyone pretended to hate that the mayor got Hinnewatcha listed as one of Travel & Leisure's Best Small Towns in America last year, but in reality, it was only a matter of time before everyone discovered the charming Vermont village. It seemed fitting that even a crisp fall day like this couldn't defeat the heaviness Maria kept trying to outrun. *I suppose it comes with the murder territory,* she thought, and forced out a laugh she didn't feel.

Isa always knows when I've cried. She breathed in deep, drawing in the comforting scent of cinnamon embedded in her skin from last night's spice run. The picket fence gate leading to her daughter's school creaked when Maria opened it. Isabelle waved, her dark, thick curls an exact match to Maria's, and she bounded down the steps to meet her mom in a fast, tight hug.

"Finally won the spitting contest against Chelsea Baker," her daughter said by way of greeting. "It went at least two inches past hers."

"Huh. Well, that's great news then, kid," Maria said, wondering how many days this particular competition would last between Isa and the Mayor's daughter. The pair were bloodthirsty competitors, the kind of not-quite friends but not-quite enemies that can come with girlhood.

"Yeah, well, I've been practicing ever since she beat me at the stick jumping," Isa said.

Isa walked backwards down the sidewalk, bouncing a little while she filled Maria in on everything that happened at school without mentioning a word about what she was learning. She'd sewn another patch on her Cat & Jack jeans at some point. The smiley faces and peace signs matched the rose colored *Love* shirt, which was stained a touch with what looked like jelly. Isa fiddled with her backpack straps as she carried on about school, her wide, gap-toothed smile and pink hoodie a harsh juxtaposition from the burn scars on her knuckles.

Maria blocked out the hint of that memory, focusing instead on the cloudless sky ahead of them. *Never again, mija.* Her mother's words flitted through her mind and she tried to think about anything else. When Isa finally took a breath in her monologue, Maria interrupted, "Look, *nena*! They strung the lights for the pumpkin patch."

Isa replied, "About time. It's almost Halloween!"

"Don't let Cate hear you say that, she'll have a stroke," Maria said as she shouldered their front door open. "I swear I think she already has an eye twitch from the amount of times people have requested a pumpkin spice anything this week."

Despite the sticking door, her peaceful living room was

a welcome sight. Every time Dave fell asleep in a drunken stupor or stayed out at his brother's house, Maria would light a few candles in the broken fireplace and add to the list that now hung on the refrigerator door. The projects ranged from painting the front door yellow (which Dave would have hated) to building a glass greenhouse out back for her plants (which Dave would have trashed). *Stop thinking about him,* she thought as she tossed her keys in the misshapen heart bowl Isa made in PreK.

"Make yourself a snack, Isa, then homework. I need to make more pumpkin spice for Cate tonight, wanna help?"

An unintelligible noise of affirmation came from somewhere in the kitchen as Isa rifled through whatever food they had leftover from the neighbors. Casseroles crowded the fridge, the food a way of saying, "I'm sorry your piece of shit husband is dead, I hope you like cheesy rice," by her neighbors.

"Did those lesbians bring you more food?"

"Jesus on a stick!" Maria exclaimed, hand on her chest. She hadn't even heard her mother pull in the drive, let alone come inside. "When did you get here? And stop with the lesbian comments, Mama. For the hundredth time, their names are Cindy and Eveline."

"Watch your mouth. And I came as soon as I could because of this," Rosa Cruz shoved her bejeweled pink phone in front of Maria's face to reveal a photo of a man.

Handsome in a too-pretty way, the man in the photo was looking into the distance in a manner akin to a retro Olan Mills pose. She wondered if that was meant to be a joke. The blonde was probably in his early forties, hair coiffed in a way that only a professional could manage and his tan a little too even to be real. "Dead Don't Lie" was written at the bottom, and Maria braced herself for what would come next.

"Shane Bolles, *mija. The* Shane Bolles is coming here," her mother waggled the phone in front of her to emphasize her point, gold and silver bangles jangling with each shift. Rosa stood 5ft, 1in but sometimes Maria swore she was 6ft 3in.

"So I heard. But, so what? Dave died of an accidental drug overdose. Case closed," Maria said. She looked anywhere but into her mother's narrowing hazel eyes. "Sounds like the guy is coming to town for an easy win."

Rosa grunted the same way that infuriated Maria as a young girl, somehow morphing the sound into an accusation and a guilt trip without words. Maria refused the bait, and they stared at each other in the silence.

Her mother broke first.

"I'm moving here," Rosa announced, arms folded.

"Hard pass, Mama."

"I'm serious, *mija.* This is trouble. You're a widow now, this house is falling apart, Isa is eating trash, *again*, now this man is about to come here, and—"

Maria held up her hand, no amount of breathing could calm her now. "Enough. You are not moving in with me now, Mama. I know what you're doing."

"Isa is barely holding it together," Rosa tried, but it sounded more like a hopeful guess than an accusation.

"Isa is happier in the last week than she was in the last two years." She held her hands out, trying to think of a way to slow her mother down. "Look, I know I made a mistake marrying him, but it's over now. We need to move on, but we need to move on without… whatever it is you're trying to do."

"No."

"No? What do you mean, 'no?' This is my home, Mama, I,"

Rosa crossed her arms across her hot pink blouse and stomped her heeled feet shoulder-width apart. She was a petite Latina barricade, immobile and relentless. *I don't have the energy for this,* Maria thought. She begrudgingly waved a white flag.

"One week, mama."

"Three months," Rosa shot back as fast as a cannon.

"Mama, this house is tiny."

She observed her lacquered nails and cocked an eyebrow at her daughter. "And a wreck."

Maria ground her teeth together, longing for the patch of sunlit grass waiting for her in the backyard and a hot cup of yerba mate. "You can stay here until this Shane Bolles business goes away. But the moment Mama," Maria ignored the smile of victory on her mother's face, "the second that man goes away and Dave's case is put to rest, you go home."

"Deal."

I gave in too soon. Maria snatched her favorite chipped mug, the one with yellow flowers, off the shelf and put the kettle on to boil. Rosa's heels clicked over, and she leaned a trim hip against the butcher block countertop to face Maria head on.

"I am living here soon enough," she began without warning, smile at hand. "I'm old, and getting feeble and you have to take care of me."

"If you're so old, stop wearing those heels, Mama." Maria raised her eyebrows in a pointed look at the tips of death her mother insisted on wearing.

"What? And then give up lipstick? I will be buried in heels, *mija*. Best you remember that."

Maria chuckled, the faint eucalyptus aroma from the tea leaves easing the tension in the room and in her shoulders. She and her mother worked their way into an amiable truce over the past few months after what felt like a decade of anger since she left home. Maria's thirty-five years felt more like a hundred and five when she thought back to her rash nineteen-year-old self, hell bent on following a boy that was definitely not worth it to the other side of the country. She didn't want to admit that her mother had been right about Dave as well. She half-listened as Rosa rattled off news about her aunt and cousins back in New York, debating if she should ever tell her what really happened to Dave. Wondering if she already knew in that innate spidey-sense mothers had about their daughters.

She dried her hands on a Dia de Los Muertos tea towel she found at the flea market. "I'm going to sit in the backyard, *alone*, Mama, until I finish my tea. Then, I'll get your bags out of the car."

"Bien. I'll find a hairbrush. I saw Isabelle's hair; I can't believe you let her go to school like that."

And so it begins.

Maria stalked outside to the concrete bistro table. The table had a giant gash down the center of it, but it was sturdy enough for a teacup. The wildflowers and grasses Maria cultivated billowed around her. Soon the browning flowerheads would need to be trimmed. For the moment, though, Maria sat in her small garden paradise, tea in hand and sun above, and began her mental list:

Get Shane Bolles off this case.

Bury Dave.

Send Mama back to New York.

She sipped the tea and assured herself, *You already killed Dave. The rest of this should be easy.*

2

THE DEAD DON'T LIE

"Dad, I think you're good on the foundation," Emily said, backpack in lap. "Besides, we're gonna be late. Chop, chop."

Shane Bolles wiggled his fingers, searching for a napkin or something other than his pants to wipe his hands. "It's sunscreen, and we have time."

"It's tinted, and you don't need a primer for sunscreen."

He ignored her, stretching his face in the mirror and testing the wrinkles that had formed overnight at his eyes. He smoothed down the sides of his hair. Airports were rife with paparazzi, and God knows what happened the last time he left in a rush.

Daily Beast: They're just like us! Dead Don't Lie *star Shane Bolles looks like the dead in Trader Joe's.*

"Buckle up, buttercup, it's gonna be a fast ride," Shane said, backing out of the driveway of their modern bungalow and avoiding a jogger.

Emily asked, "So, what's this guy's name?"

"Grandpa? I don't know. What do you want to call him?" Shane said, easing into traffic.

"No. Like, what's the dead guy's name?"

"What dead guy?"

Emily held up Shane's phone. "The guy Uncle Frankie sent. Isn't that why we're going to Hinnewatcha?"

Shane attempted to grab his phone but Emily, in all her 14-year-old glory, was quicker to the draw.

"Hands free, Dad. You can't afford another ticket."

He replied, "Mind your own. And your elders. And then read me that text."

Emily read, *"Don't kill me Shane. But it was too good to pass up. Dead guy in your hometown, right when you were already heading there."*

"This time, I really am going to kill him. There are too many agents in LA anyway, no one will miss him," Shane said.

"You always say Frankie is more like a brother than your agent," Emily argued, "And besides, why else would we go there, if not for a case?"

Shane maneuvered onto the freeway. "I specifically told Frankie that we— I mean, I—that *I* needed some time."

Emily's mouth dropped open, "Oh. My. God. Dad. Tell me this isn't because of school. I thought we were done with that."

"No," Shane said, adamantly shaking his head.

"Oh my God! You're doing the face!"

Shane dropped the exaggerated frown, schooling his face to neutral. "I needed a break, Buttercup," he stole a glance at his rapidly angering teen and decided to just rip the band-aid off. "And uh, you know, a break could be good for both of us right now. LA is so smoggy. I swear it's making my wrinkles worse."

Emily, despite the abundance of freckles and her tendency to still hop when she was mad, was a force to be reckoned with when she lost her cool. Shane tried not to envision the headlines if someone decided to film them in this traffic. *Shane Bolles, read the riot act by teenage daughter on the 405.*

He let her waves of teenage angst roll over him, wondering if the dead guy in Hinnewatcha was someone he knew. *I can't believe Frankie did this. He knew I was going back to Vermont for a break. I specifically told him—no cases. No interviews. No photo ops.*

Emily's rant ran its course into indignant silence by the time they got to LAX. They rushed to their gate, late as usual, and her death dagger stares were enough to make him grateful that the airline seated them across the aisle from each other and not right next to each other.

Shane gave Emily his best smile, but she just shoved her headphones over her ears. *She'll be fine by the time we get to the east coast.* Shane connected to the wifi and googled the name Frankie sent despite his best attempts to ignore it. A man in his mid-forties, dough-faced with angry eyes looked back at him from the photo on his screen. *Dave Fever. That's a good name, I would have remembered that if he was in school with me.* The man in the photo stood next to his wife according to the fine print. She managed to make a tepid smile look more dreary than a frown. *They look miserable.*

Why would they use this photo? He read through the first article from the Voracious Vermonter:

Hinnewatcha, VT — David Fever, 42, was found dead in his home September 20th, 2023. The investigation is ongoing; police have not announced if foul play is suspected. Fever is survived by his wife of two years, Maria Fever, his step-daughter, Isabelle, and his older brother Greg Fever. Fever was a longtime resident of Hinnewatcha, and an assistant manager at The Potted Soil garden center. He was offered a full ride to UVM for hockey until a knee injury took him out of the game his senior year. No known—

"Excuse me," the woman sitting next to him said, interrupting his reading. Shane sat a little straighter, selfie-smile at the ready.

"Yes?"

"Can I scoot by?" She asked. "Too much water."

"Oh, right. Yep."

Emily snorted from across the aisle, "You thought she wanted a photo, didn't you?"

"Absolutely not," Shane lied.

He got into his signature pose from the *Dead Don't Die* title sequence just as his seat mate walked back, but she just paused uncomfortably and shimmied past his knees. Emily laughed outright then, and he knew they'd be OK by the time they got to Vermont.

***

The road to Hinnewatcha ambled past rolling farmland and through russet colored forests, the pavement dark with a recent rain. Shane lowered the windows so the cool, bonfire-

17

tinged air could breeze in, and nestled into the rental car's seat warmers. They listened to the local radio at first, but the commercials were so obnoxious even Emily didn't object when he muted it in favor of the white noise of the drive.

By the time they reached his dad's farm, fog had rolled in from the mountains and settled into the treetops under a low harvest moon. Somewhere across the hills, a dog barked, but otherwise coming home sounded like the exact kind of quiet Shane fled more than 20 years before.

"This place is unreal," Emily said, "I can't believe you hated it."

Shane grabbed a bag from the trunk, grunting. "Gee-whiz, kid, how much did you pack? And I never said I hated it."

"That's your bag, Dad, and you always said you hated it here. I distinctly remember a line about 'bugs and dirt floors,'" Emily said. She turned to take in the wide yard and the farmhouse painted Venetian red like so many barns in Vermont. "You made it sound like you grew up in a shack."

"Is that what he told you?" His dad's voice sounded different in person. The same boom he remembered, but clearer than the handful of terse conversations they'd had in the last decade.

Emily, loyal to the bone, stayed next to Shane's side as he turned to face his dad for the first time in 23 years. Age hadn't softened Brandon Bolles' broad shoulders, and he stood arms crossed in the porch light as stoic as the last time Shane was home. Shane looked across the yard at his dad's still-bald head, the same thick eyebrows, and fat mustache.

Other than his facial hair fading to white, his dad looked the same. Bald and disappointed.

Shane, always quick to hug, found himself rooted to the gravel drive. Emily broke the silence first, "So, you're the asshole, huh?"

"Emily—" Shane had pictured a lot of awkward small talk and stilted silences, not the gauntlet of intros Emily just threw down. *I should have known better.*

But before he could reprimand, or make a better introduction, or jump back in the car to flee, his dad just nodded.

"You'll fit in fine in this town, granddaughter. Leave the bags for the junior asshole there. He looks like he needs a minute."

Emily looked back at Shane, the anger from two flights before gone, and nodded once as if going into battle. She grabbed her backpack and disappeared into the soft glow behind his dad. Shane wondered if he should have prepped her better. Or prepped his dad.

He followed the pair inside, and paused at the threshold. It would have been easier if the living room weren't the same. He pretended the light blue recliner wasn't there, striding by it and aiming for the belly of the house. Brandon thunked a cup of water in front of Emily, his wooden chair groaning as he sat down at the scratched up farmhouse table that served as an island when needed. Brandon Bolles heaved out a deep breath that seemed to echo in the too-quiet house.

"What's the chance you got any oat milk?" Emily asked into the awkward silence.

"Zero to none, you hippie," his dad replied. "How many tattoos do you have?"

"Only the tramp stamp," she smiled, nodding at the refrigerator. "Do we need to forage for dinner or do you have anything in that fridge?"

Shane tried to intervene but the Bolles volleying match was a bit intimidating for anyone, and he still felt a little off kilter being back in this kitchen.

"I might have some mashed potatoes and meatloaf in there if you can stomach it after the malnutrition that one," Brandon jerked his head in Shane's direction, "has forced you to endure."

Emily's smile could have frozen a trash fire. "I'm svelte, thank you very much, not malnourished, and we eat just fine."

"You're scrawny, and you talk too much."

"Jesus, Dad. Remind me why we even came here?" Emily asked, arms crossed.

Suddenly two generations of Bolles stared at him, expectantly, and he realized that for all the features Emily inherited from her mother, she got Brandon Bolles' dark green eyes. It was disconcerting.

His dad raised his coffee mug, not blinking, "I was just about to ask the same question."

Shane's chair screeched back as he stood up from the table. "Who wants meatloaf?"

"No! No one gets meatloaf until I get some goddamned answers," Brandon said, thick finger pointing at the fridge as if he could keep it closed with sheer will.

Emily launched back, "What, are you going to starve us out? Let's leave, Dad. This guy sucks worse than mom."

"Let's just eat something," Shane tried, smiling weakly. "I think we'll all feel better." He opened the fridge and started pulling plates out at random.

"Don't pussyfoot around. I haven't seen you since the funeral and I've never even met this feral cat you're calling a girl. I want to know why you called me two days ago for the first time in eight years, telling," his dad reared back to emphasize his biggest issue. *"Telling* me that you are coming here for a while and staying in *my* house."

Shane held up a hand, trying to pacify the man fuming at the end of the table, "I just thought—" But Emily cut him off mid-sentence.

"What do you mean 'you're calling a girl?' Let me guess. You have something against girls with short hair?" She fluffed her short locks. "Least I have some."

"You look like Macaulay Culkin."

Emily shook her head, "I don't even know who that is."

"You don't know who Macaulay Culkin is?" Brandon's eyes widened at Shane before turning back to his granddaughter. *"Home Alone?"*

Shane couldn't help it. He laughed. *I forgot how much he loves Macaulay Culkin.*

Brandon pointed again, "Don't laugh. I can't believe she doesn't know who Macaulay Culkin is and you live in LA. And you're obviously not feeding her, so for chrissake would you just heat up the meatloaf already?"

"Ma, meatloaf!" Shane tried, but neither Bolles got the reference. "Right. Meatloaf. In a jiffy."

He tore off plastic wrap, cringing at the feel of Saran, but almost dropped the plate when he saw the tin yellow timer on top of the microwave. Shane looked back at his dad in disbelief.

"You put *the timer* in the kitchen?" Shane shuddered.

"I use it for cookies," Brandon said, more than a touch indignant. "It is, after all, a timer."

Emily raised her hand, "What's so special about that timer?"

Brandon laughed. "Let me guess. She doesn't know? Well I can't *wait* to be a part of this conversation. Why don't you ask the more important question here, Feral Cat?"

"And what is that, Old Man?" Emily retorted.

"Ask your dad how he *really* solves all those cold cases." Brandon leaned back, mustache widening over his first genuine smile like an accordion unfolding.

Shane looked at the cold plate of meatloaf in his hand. *If I smash this into my face, it might startle them both enough to slow down the shit storm that is about to occur.*

"What, that he Raises the dead and asks them?" Emily replied, "Old news, Old Man. What else you got?"

Shane sighed. *This is going to be a long night.* "I'll get the mashed potatoes."

3

Chit Chats with the Dead

SHANE WOKE UP TANGLED in the blue-green flannel sheets he'd slept in as a teenager. He still felt too big for the bed, and the same black and white Joe Strummer poster greeted him in the midmorning light. Bacon sizzled downstairs, and an unexpected moment of grief squeezed his chest. It was as if he could hear his mom downstairs even years later.

The tableside war his dad and Emily waged last night felt days, not hours away, and despite his best effort at reasoning his way into staying in bed, he couldn't avoid the inevitable. He grabbed his too-full doc kit from his duffel and proceeded through his morning routines of facial care that seemed to get longer each year. By the time he ducked down the stairs, careful not to hit his head on the low ceiling, the bacon had made it to the table.

Emily shoveled scrambled eggs into her mouth, watching her grandfather out of the corner of her eye. Her hair was askew and she wore her favorite fuzzy socks that he bought her two Christmases ago in Santa Monica.

"Morning. How'd you sleep?" Shane asked, kissing her head.

Brandon didn't even turn from the stovetop. "I'm surprised your daughter can sleep at all given that she's seen the dead rise up to talk to you just so you can feel important."

"Yes, I would love some coffee, thank you so much for asking," Shane said under his breath.

He was reminded that his dad had freakishly good hearing when Brandon replied, "Like I told your lovely hippie daughter, this is not a diner. Get it yourself." He pointed the greasy spatula at the coffee pot.

"I just asked if he had any yogurt or fruit, " Emily said. "I didn't realize it was going to make him go crazy."

"Mad doesn't even come close to what I'm feeling, Feral Cat, and it has nothing to do with your stupid request for yogurt." Brandon tossed the spatula in the sink, clanging against the other dirty dishes and faced Shane. "What in the hell would make you think it's ok to take her *with you* to a Raising? She's 14. Do you really think showing a little girl a zombie is a great idea? You were 17 before your mom even hinted at what she could do."

"Ok, well, now who's being dramatic? You know the dead we Raise are not anything like zombies, first. And second, yes, I did think it was a good idea to tell her sooner. It's better that she sees a Raising with me a few times so it's not so intimidating when she has to do one on her own. And she knows she won't come into her abilities anyway until she's 17."

Brandon tossed his hands up. "This is what I tried to

tell your mother. When does someone ever *really* need to raise a dead person?"

Shane's head started to pound behind his eyes. "We went through this last night. It's a great responsibility passed down from generation—"

"No. Your mother tried to make that same argument but I swear she only Raised people that had good gossip," Brandon said. "I know better. You didn't want anything with your," he fluttered his hand in the air before he stammered out, "—your ability—until you figured out how you could make money off it."

"And there it is." Shane said, heart pounding and bacon roiling in his belly. "You resent me for making more money and having a better life than what you have. Well *I'm* sorry."

"No, you idiot. I am mad because you only take low-hanging cases and cut corners instead of doing real police work. I am mad because you're teaching an arcane, unnecessary, and unnatural ritual to a little girl so what—you can feel special together? And now you come home, ready to bring all the big shot cameras into my house so you can look like a hero for solving a case any Hinnewatchan with eyes could solve?"

"I did not come here to Raise Dave Fever. That was just a coincidence."

Brandon asked, "Then why? Why come here now for the first time in 20-something years?"

"Because," Shane started. He thought about just telling them both the truth. But Emily was wearing the fuzzy socks, and despite the chaos of his life with her, she was still his little girl. He had to protect her.

"You're right, Dad. I thought the Dave Fever case would be easy." Shane tried not to let his dad's disappointed look weigh on him, and he lied again, because that was what he really did best. "I need some quick cash and this will sell well. We'll be out soon enough, I can see that this was a mistake."

Brandon turned, done with the conversation.

"Come on Emily," Shane said, dropping the bacon in the trash. "I'll show you around town and you can use the Wifi at Mama Cate's. The wifi was terrible here even a decade ago, and I can't imagine it's improved. Nothing ever changes."

***

Maria balanced the canisters of pumpkin spice between the crook of one arm and her chin as she hipped the car door shut. Her too-long-to-be-bangs were weeks overdue for a trim and blocked the only visibility between the canisters in her arms. She didn't see Greg until it was too late.

"Only two weeks and you're already forgetting me, little sister?"

She shifted her haul to the side, "Greg. Sorry, didn't see you. Everything alright?"

What a stupid question, Maria. His brother's dead. As usual, she couldn't quite say the right thing to Dave's older brother. He unnerved her with the way he seemed to be waiting for her to say or do the wrong thing. *If he only knew.*

Greg never smiled, he smirked. He was leaner than Dave ever was, gaunt at the cheekbones and hairline high on his pale forehead. Seeing him without an oversized Carhartt beanie on his head was as bizarre as talking to him in public. The two generally avoided each other. Though, now, she wondered if avoiding him was something only she did.

"Yea, it finally feels like things are going to be alright," Greg said. One side of his face tipped up in that half smirk that never reached the scar under his eye. He reached for the canisters, tattooed knuckles close to her face. Maria had to check herself from flinching away as he took one. "Have you heard the news? Fancy TV detective is gonna find out who did this. That joke of a cop will finally get his ass handed to him."

Maria didn't feel like it was the time to correct him. Levi was the police chief now, not just a cop. She also didn't want to linger any longer. She nodded her head for him to walk with her and started making her way to Mama Cate's. *Slow, Maria, you're not running.*

She empathized with the woman that gave Greg a wide berth on the sidewalk. "I heard about that," Maria said. "Dave and I never got Bravo, though, so I don't know anything about the guy. Glad he's here. It'll be nice to get some closure and lay Dave to rest." When Greg didn't respond she couldn't help but fill the dead air. "Do you want to come with me to the parlor to pick out an urn for Dave's ashes this week?"

"We aren't cremating him."

Shit. "Ah, you sure? Dave always said he didn't like the idea of his body falling apart in the earth." Maria had no idea what Dave would have wanted, but giving anything back to the earth sounded like something he would have raged against. She could almost hear him, *"Another thing that just takes something from me."*

"Nah," Greg continued. "I'll scatter his ashes with our other brother at the farm at some point, but not yet."

"Farm" was a polite word for the littered dirt patch between broken down RVs and tireless cars outside of Hinnewatcha where Greg lurked. They were almost to Cate's, and though Maria really didn't want to continue this conversation, it was better to do so in public. She needed Dave cremated as fast as possible, and the past two weeks already felt like an eternity.

Greg continued before she could push it, "The detective will want a look at his body before he's buried. Especially since the lab at Memorial didn't find enough drugs to cause an overdose."

She stumbled over the weathered brick sidewalk. *How in the hell did Greg hear that before I did?* Chills slid down Maria's body and she clutched the canisters tighter to her chest. She said, calmer than she would have thought possible, "I thought you found him next to an empty syringe?"

"Don't be so stupid, Maria," Greg snorted. "Dave knew his limits. He wouldn't have taken more than he could handle. I've said so since we found him. It wasn't an overdose."

Maria was grateful for whomever caught Greg's eye over her shoulder. Or at least she was until Greg smirked.

"And there he is," Greg said, nodding once for Maria to turn. "Detective Bolles!"

Cate's front door never felt so far away. She turned back around to face the man her mother warned her about, the one that could very well ruin her life. He was farther off than she anticipated, the white bell tower of Town Hall gleaming behind him, as if he was an apostle sent from God to banish her to hell.

Shane Bolles walked with his hands in the pockets of well tailored jeans, his white V-neck sweater pristine. Brass blond hair that curled at the ends matched the short, choppy locks of the girl who walked beside him. Detective Bolles stood a couple of feet taller than Maria, his height only emphasized more when he finally came within arms reach.

Greg nodded his head up and down as if this man were walking towards them to arrest Maria on the spot and give him all the vindication he'd been searching for in life. "Detective Bolles!" He repeated.

For a moment, Shane Bolles looked wary, but the flash of a bright smile happened so fast that Maria wondered if she imagined it. She clutched the remaining canister in her arms like a lifeline.

Shane said, 'That's me. What's your name?"

The leather cuff of Shane's slim watch shifted as he stuck his right hand out. The squeaky clean J. Crew look gave way to something else as a tattoo of a small, red thread wrapped around his wrist became visible.

A memory of Lita popped into Maria's head when she saw the tattoo. Maria was just tall enough to reach her grandmother's counter, and she stretched high on her toes as Lita's liver spotted hands tied a thin, red string around her wrist.

"Mal de Ojo,"

Greg and the detective stopped speaking mid-sentence, and Maria flushed at the realization that she'd spoken aloud.

Shane's pale grey eyes focused on Maria, "Come again?"

"Sorry, nothing." She shook her head. "You were saying?"

The girl, maybe a couple years older than Isa, looked at her like she had sprouted horns from her nose.

"Ah," Shane said, his eyes crinkling with an easy smile. "I was saying that it's nice to be back home. And fortunate, well not fortunate because he died, but fortuitous that I am here when a murder occurred."

All the good energy and calm focus Maria tried to cultivate with self help podcasts and books fled. *Murder. Murderer.* The man's affable smile faltered and he glanced down at the girl at his side.

Maria reeled herself back in, every ounce of willpower poured into not falling apart and confessing on the sidewalk. "Murder? No. Dave overdosed. Accidentally, of course. He loved his life. Full of joy." *Stop talking Maria,* "Happy, seemed like he really was excited about his future, and what he could give back." *Just stop.* "No one thinks it was murder."

"It was 100% a murder." Greg went on as if she hadn't spoken. "That's why I reached out to you on your website. I just never thought you'd come so fast."

The detective's smile widened, his perfect white teeth on full display. "That's why we're here. To get down to the bottom of Dave Fever's death. Now, if you'll excuse us, we have a lot that needs to be done before we can get started."

Maria took the other spice canisters back from Greg. "Yay."

She walked into Mama Cate's, repeating in her head like a mantra now, *Get Shane Bolles off this case.*

***

"Well that was weird," Emily said. She fired up her laptop and blew the steam off her mug of Mama Cate's hot chocolate.

They took a table wedged in between two bookcases, which at least shielded Shane from too many prying eyes. He ignored the handful of customers looking a touch too casual as they walked past their table a second time.

"What part?" He asked, glancing again at Maria as she worked the counter. It was disconcerting to admit that a potential murderer was attractive. He shimmied his chair over to face Emily and the back of the store instead.

"Did you not see her face?" Emily replied, "Dave's wife, or widow or whatever. When you said 'murder' she looked like she was about to faint."

"Well she *is* freshly widowed, kid. Can't blame her."

"You saw the photos that Frankie sent. She definitely hated him. I didn't think it was possible for someone to look so miserable in a wedding photo. And who could blame her? I even got the ick from looking at him."

Shane tried to prioritize his questions and reign in Emily's imagination. "Back up. The what? What is the ick?"

Emily shuddered. "The ick. Like some creepy guy looks at you too long or like you kiss someone with too much spit in their mouth."

"Gross. Wait, you've been kissed?" Shane asked. "By who?"

She rolled her eyes. "We're not going there. Stay focused."

"Do you need me to say something? Did someone force

31

themselves on you?" *I could be back in LA by tomorrow night.* "Just give me a name, I won't make it weird. Who are the parents?"

"Ohmygod stop. Reel it in." Emily said, looking over her shoulder as if all of Mama Cate's was listening. "First, you make everything weird. And second, no one forced themself on me. If someone did, I'd hit them with a chair. And, yes, I've been kissed. I'm in 9th grade, Dad, lots of people have kissed, so don't look at me like that. Now, focus. We have a murder to deal with and I'm not telling you who anyway."

Shane crossed his arms and the pair had a silent standoff at the table.

Emily always won.

"Fine," he said, tabling that conversation for a later time when he could get to the bottom of which scrawny kid in her class put the moves on her. "Let's say Maria was unhappy. There are a lot of options for someone to get out of a marriage that doesn't involve murdering one's spouse."

But even as Shane said it, he agreed with Emily. *There's something off.* He put his head in his hands, rubbing his eyes. Resigned, he took a deep breath and said, "OK. I'll have Frankie set up a meet and greet with the police and coordinate a time with Dave Fever's body."

Emily clapped, a bit too giddy at the prospect of talking to a dead person. "I can't wait. Can I film it?"

"Ohmygod, no. We've talked about this. Absolute, hard no. The only reason I ever brought you to a Raising was so you wouldn't pee yourself like I did the first time I Raised solo. But, you can never film it. No one, and I mean absolutely no one, can know what our family can do."

"But why? There's weirder stuff going on. The news basically acknowledged that UFOs are real and yet still no one cares. It'll make your life a lot easier."

"Buttercup, I'm pushing it with the show as it is," Shane said. "It's a tool that could be used for good, like we do with solving cases, or bad."

He thought back to the night of the van, rubbing his neck where the bag had been tied over his head.

Shane grabbed Emily's hand, "Promise me, kid. No filming, no telling anyone—ever—what we can do. Otherwise, I won't teach you and I'll let it die with me."

"Fine. But how come you told Frankie?"

"Frankie is the absolute last person I'd tell. He's an agent. No one talks more than agents in LA and he would 100% turn that into a new TV show. And then a book. And then a board game, and a puzzle. It would never end."

Emily slumped down in her chair. "Oh. I always just thought he knew." She pulled her headphones out of her backpack and nodded once to him. "You should call the police chief now though to get access if we're going to Raise Dave soon."

Shane looked around for his cell phone, patting down his pockets and looking under the table. "Damnit. Be right back."

The coffee shop/wine bar/bookstore/post office was as busy as he remembered as a kid. Bookshelves took up the back half of the room, with tables and chairs scattered in between them and the long counter that ran the length of the store. The barista counter doled out coffee and the wine from the left end, closest to the door, and the packages piled up on the far right side near the scale. He slid between the locals milling around and spotted the phone he'd left in no-man's land between the packages and the espresso machine.

He touched the shoulder of the man blocking him from the counter. "Excuse me, I just need to grab my phone."

The man turned and the frown already present on his face deepened when he looked at Shane. "Great. As if I don't have enough problems on my hands. I suppose you're the one I should thank for the 6 a.m. phone call from our mayor?"

"Sorry? Have we met?" Shane asked.

The glowering man held a coffee in one hand and put his other in his pocket, ignoring Shane's outstretched hand. "Levi Madison, the Police Chief and the detective working Dave Fever's case. I'm an *actual* detective, about to wrap up the *real* report, and yet I got a phone call saying I have to drag this out so your camera crew can film you 'solving the case'."

He somehow managed to make air quotes look menacing. Shane replied, "Look, if you've got this solved, we don't need to keep this going. I'll explain to my producers that we got here too late and that it's closed." *Then Emily and I can just lie low and no one from LA will know that we're here.*

The chief watched him without responding for what felt like forever. Shane felt the first trickle of sweat down the back of his merino sweater and he caught Maria's honey brown eyes across the counter. Finally the police chief spoke. "Wish I could. But the Mayor is insistent, so we're going to make this fast."

***

Maria fiddled with the steamer, trying to not be obvious as she eavesdropped on Shane Bolles and Levi's conversation on the other side of the counter. The sight of the two of them together made her already nervous stomach roil. *I'm not going to throw up. They're just talking.* Shane caught her eyes as Levi said something she couldn't hear. *Nope, they're plotting. I'm going to lose Isa. I'm going to jail. I will never see the sun. I will never—*

Someone opened the door to Mama Cate's, the tingling bell scattering her panicked thoughts for a moment. The man that walked in was lean, wiry in a way that gave Maria the impression of a ferret. His dark hair, olive skin, and coffee colored eyes could have come from anywhere, but the tattoos across his neck and on the sides of his face screamed LA. Maria spent the previous decade dodging any man that looked like the one that just walked in, and yet she felt this overwhelming urge to pay attention to him. *Get it together, Maria. What is wrong with you?*

She dried the thick, cream-colored mugs with her towel and watched the newcomer out of the corner of her eye. He looked around the packed seating area. Some of the locals moved unsubtly out of the way when he started to move through the small crowd towards the bookshelves. He glanced over at Maria and stilled, though his eyes didn't catch hers. Instead, he seemed to be watching Levi and Shane. The stranger smiled and Maria couldn't help but shiver.

Maria ignored her instincts only once in her life. The day Dave Fever announced that he wanted to marry her, she said yes, instead of a resounding hell no. She thought she'd warm up to Dave. She thought marriage would make him softer. She thought the safety of this town required a man, someone to help care for her and Isa unlike the spectacularly disappointing men she'd left in LA. But her gut told her then that saying yes was a terrible idea and yet she ignored it all the way to the altar. That eventually led to the disaster of her life as it was known today.

Now, her gut told her that the newcomer was not here for her, but for one of the two men on the other side of the counter. *Help him, mijita.* Her grandmother Lita's voice, clear as the bell on the front door, rang through her mind. Maria didn't think, she just acted as the newcomer reached into his pocket.

"Oh! I can't believe I forgot! Guys," she snapped her fingers across the counter and into Shane and Levi's conversation. "Yep, you two. Need some help in the back."

Chief Madison scowled at her, and Shane looked understandably confused. It didn't stop Maria's half-thought-out plan. "Right now!"

Cate side-eyed Maria from the register, but for once in her life didn't say anything. The men followed Maria around the counter and through the swinging door. She glanced back where the newcomer was moments before, but she didn't see him in the crowd.

"What's the problem Mrs. Fever?" Levi asked.

Maria was atrocious at lying. *Why did I ever think I could kill someone and get away with it?* "Soooooo," she scrambled, trying to think of what would have prompted her to bring them back here as she fidgeted with her grandmother's ring.

"I heard that Dave's toxicology report came back." *What are you doing? That is the worst thing you can bring up to these two men.*

Levi gave the stilted silence he seemed to give every question before he responded. "How did you hear that? I don't even have a copy of that report yet."

Fabulous, Maria. Bring up the husband you murdered to two detectives and make them even more suspicious. Maria twisted the pearl and gold band over and over around her middle finger until she noticed Shane watching her hands. She shoved them into the deep pockets of her cardigan. "I ran into Greg before my shift. He's the one that told me. I just assumed you knew?"

Levi pulled his cell phone from his back pocket, thumbing the screen before looking at Maria and then Shane, his perpetual frown growing. "How did he get that report?"

Both Shane and Maria shrugged simultaneously. Shane responded first, "Who is Greg?"

"Greg is my late husband's brother," Maria said, stealing a glance out the small portal window to the rest of the shop. The man that set off all her internal bells was out of eyesight. "You just met him outside?" Maria said.

Levi stood taller, feet shoulder width apart. "Really? You just got in town, haven't even come by the station, and you're already out there stirring up problems and talking to relatives?"

Shane opened his mouth but Maria beat him to it. "No, Greg just happened to be outside with me when Detective Bolles walked up."

"Maria," Levi said before pausing to correct himself. "I'm sorry, Mrs. Fever. I haven't had the chance to review the toxicology report. Clearly. I don't know what's on it, I don't know why Greg Fever would ever get that report before me, and I don't know why this man," he nodded his head in Detective Bolles' direction, "would ever need to be involved in this case. But there's more to your husband's death than I gave it credit before. Please accept my sincere apologies for making you think it was an accidental overdose pre-emptively."

Maria felt like at any moment she'd catch on fire, burn through the floorboards, and go straight to hell, bypassing the court and judicial system entirely. *I'm going to throw up on Shane Bolles' pristine loafers,* she thought.

Levi continued, "I've been asked to allow Mr. TV Detective here a few days to review the case files. But, given that he's not a real detective—" Shane opened his mouth as if to defend himself, but Levi pushed on. "—he's just a TV personality, we don't have to give him, or his producers, *anything* regarding Dave Fever's death. However, since it sounds like I've overlooked something, I'm willing to swallow my pride and let someone else take a second look at this. But I won't do it without your permission. Do you want Detective Bolles to review this case?"

Maria couldn't believe her luck. She could say no. Shane Bolles had no jurisdiction here. She could get him out of Hinnewatcha with just a word, right now. She even thought for a moment Shane Bolles shook his head no as well, but she couldn't be sure. *But that won't get Levi off this case. And it won't bury Dave any faster if Levi has to look into why drugs*

didn't kill Dave. If I say no, won't that be even more suspicious?
Is this a test?

She didn't have the ability to let pauses in conversations linger... let alone pauses in conversations hinged on her response about her murdered husband. So she went with her gut, and said, "OK. Let's let Detective Bolles take a look at this."

She wondered later that night if her instincts had finally let her down.

4

Buckle Up, Buttercup

EVERY BUILDING HAS A back door, including the morgue at Memorial. In LA, there were so many doctors and staff at the hospital, no one ever cared if a new face showed up in scrubs to wheel a dead body. But even in the bigger city outside of Hinnewatcha, someone would've said something about a newcomer pushing a cadaver.

Which is why Shane ignored the guilt in his gut as he picked the lock under Emily's scrutiny. In her defense, she was alarmed at the breaking-and-entering part. But she was oddly calm about the seeing-a-dead-person bit of the night. Emily scanned the loading dock area, turning her head at every noise, but they were alone except for a few large trash cans and an empty gurney. Fortunately, the exterior security camera was still askew thanks to Shane's nudge during his "official" visit earlier in the day.

The lock clicked, no alarm sounded, and the pair walked into the well lit hallway, clipboards in hand in case someone approached them. He led Emily to the unmarked bright yellow door and used the key fob he'd swiped earlier to get inside. The office where Shane had read the medical examiner's notes with his TV crew earlier was dark.

Emily whispered, "I thought morgues kept their dead people in a bunch of drawers in the wall?"

Shane shook his head, trying not to inhale the warring smells of formaldehyde and disinfectant. "Small and old hospitals like this one just use walk-ins. Not too far off from what a supermarket uses." He pointed to the cooler in the corner, "They pulled Dave from the second one earlier. Give me a hand."

The pair wheeled the nearest gurney over and opened the stainless steel fridge aptly labeled "The Chiller" per an old placard at its side. "D. Fever" was scrawled on a tag outside of his black body bag on the bottom shelf. Shane and Emily half pulled, half pushed his heavy body onto the gurney, its wheels squeaking in protest.

Shane said, "Grab my bag and meet me by the examiner's table. Remember what we practiced?"

"We didn't practice anything about the Raising!" Emily whisper-panicked. Her fair skin took on a translucent glow under the harsh medical lighting and lime green tiled walls. The blue windbreaker with the "Integrity Transport" patch on the arm kept slipping off her slim shoulders.

"No, not the Raising," Shane said, trying to keep her calm. "What do we say if someone walks in?"

"Oh right. We're with Integrity Transport, here to take Dave Fever's body to the cargo plane so he can be buried in New Jersey."

"You can be bored, agitated, annoyed, or indifferent. But you can't be guilty," he said.

Emily rolled her eyes, "I'm not an idiot."

"That's the face, Buttercup, good job." He wheeled the body and said over his shoulder, "Now bring me the salt."

Shane tried not to gag as he opened the body bag to Dave Fever's pallid, naked body. He checked the ankle ID, *Won't make that mistake again,* and reached for the large ziplock bag Emily handed over.

"K, kiddo, a few basics. First, freshly grated black sea salt works best but you can make do with some Morton's in a pinch." Shane piled the black salt in a thick line from Dave's weak chin down his chest, making a face at the lint gathered as he pooled more salt into his belly button.

"What's the difference between Morton's and this stuff?"

Shane motioned to the bundle of herbs while answering. "Longevity. Morton's will only give you 10 seconds or so. This stuff, which has charcoal in it and some other ingredients I probably should know, gives us a full minute, if we're lucky." He pried open Dave's stiff mouth just wide enough to shove the flat leaf in.

"White sage, just one piece, goes in the mouth. Too much and they'll spend the full minute coughing it up. Not enough and they won't remember how to speak. Now, crushed sumac goes on every fingertip," he said as he put the ziplock bag of red powder on Dave's forehead. "This is so they keep their hands at their sides."

Emily's eyes were wide as she scribbled notes with a fluffy purple pen, its tip catching in Dave Fever's dark arm hair. "What happens if you forget it?"

Shane looked anywhere but Emily's eyes. "Mom always told me it's because they're clumsy and knock everything off the table."

"And?"

Shane frowned deeper, raising his shoulders in a protracted shrug.

"You're doing the face," she said, jabbing the fluffy pen at him. "What are you not telling me?"

"Well, it uh–" He struggled with balancing telling her too much and having her flip out, and not telling her enough, which could set her up for a disaster later. *She needs to remember this.* "It helps remind the dead person not to hurt you." He wiggled his own sumac coated fingers at the corpse and spoke in the cartoon pitch that always had her cackling as a little girl, "Helloooo there Mr. Fever, we're friends! Don't hurt us!"

It didn't work.

Emily's eyes widened even further and she took a step back. "Hurt us? You never told me that they could hurt you. Has that ever happened before? Is it gonna happen this time?"

Shane dusted off the sumac on his pants and raised a hand, trying to calm Emily. But they were short on time and he needed to get Dave talking.

"No," He lied, grabbing the bag of sumac off Dave's face and zipping it closed. "Never. But I don't ever forget the sumac and I never go cheap on it either, just in case." Shane sprinkled ashes on the table around the perimeter of the body. "Last one. Focus. Any ash works, but cigarette ash tends to distract them, so I'd avoid it. This is to ground their soul back into their body one more time."

Emily nodded, sprinkling ash on the other side of the table. "And the chips? What are those for?"

He popped open the top. "I didn't eat lunch."

"Gross," she said, eyeing the can as if he intended to eat the Pringles off Dave's belly. He shoved a slim stack of Pringles in his mouth and tossed the can back into his bag behind him.

"Okay, here we go," Shane said over the last few chews. He raised his hands over Dave's chest, hovering them above the small mound of salt. "Now remember, the murdered ones always describe their killer first. Names if they have them."

"Maria," Emily said, without hesitation.

"We don't know it was the wife."

She crossed her arms. "Ok. *Probably* Maria."

"Enough. The murderer will be described first. Everyone wants to be vindicated, even after death. If they don't know who it was, or if it wasn't murder, they'll describe any and all details their soul grabbed on the way out."

"You think he'll be as chatty as that old biddy we brought back last time?" She asked.

"Always. I've never been around one that didn't want to talk as long as they're able to." Shane nodded to his trusty timer shaped like a tomato by the sink. "Put 60 seconds on the tomato."

"Sure I can't film this?" Emily asked, while twisting the bright red timer.

"Positive," Shane said as his hands began to emit a glowing white light.

"Record it?" She actually looked serious. "Like, just audio."

Shane lifted his hands, the glow faded. "I will send you to the car. You do not have to be part—"

Emily rolled her eyes again, "Ugh fine. Do the thing." She set the timer on the sink with a *clink.*

Shane's hands tingled as if he'd dipped them in menthol, the thrill and the fear rushing in as if this were his first Raising decades ago. He rushed through the words in a sing-song voice the way his mother taught him from rote memory. He could never get them quite right when he tried to write them down.

*These words are only meant for our mouths, my Bolley boy. Not eve*n paper can hold them.

The words and phrases fell out of his mouth, each one heavier than the last until he felt like he had to gag the final syllable out.

Dave Fever, dead a solid two weeks, sat straight up, sucking a giant gush of air into his hairy, pale chest. He pivoted his torso towards Shane, arms stuck against his sides, and the mound of black salt scattered to the ground. His naked lower half remained unmoving on the stainless steel gurney thanks to the perimeter of ash. He looked unblinkingly at Shane, but opened and closed his mouth like a fish gasping for air.

Shane knew something wasn't right in the seconds Dave just watched him, unspeaking.

"Did you mess it up?" Emily asked, popping out sideways from the other side of Dave.

The question just left her mouth when the first light

bulb shattered by the door. She yelped, startled. Shane jumped too, nerves on high alert. Then suddenly every bulb burst in quick succession in the room until the only one left was right above Dave's body.

Shane fisted the sumac in his pocket, ready in case Dave moved, as glass rained down, "Emily, get out of here! Run to the car, lock the…"

Dave Fever's voice was high, his Hinnewatchan accent thick: "Tha. Bitch." But he was cut off less than a second later as his back arched into a grotesque backbend. It was as if an invisible thread pulled his chest towards the ceiling until only the tips of his hairy toes and his shoulders touched the table. The corpse of Dave Fever opened and shut his mouth, but no more sounds emerged.

Shane and Emily both stumbled back, away from the sight before them as someone, or something, spoke out of Dave Fever's mouth. It spoke with a deep raspy voice, and syncopated cadence: "*Two more. Two more deaths to. Come before the darkened. Moon, meets the canine.*"

Dave Fever's body slammed back down on the steel gurney just as the tomato timer rang out its first tinny bleat. Shane looked up to see Emily backed up to the counter as far as she could go.

"We leave right now," Shane ordered. He grabbed the timer, but left everything else on Dave's stiff corpse. When Emily didn't move, he yanked her into the empty hallway. Pushing her ahead of him, they bolted for the double doors and out to the loading dock area where his car waited.

The rental car tires squealed and Shane eyed the rear view mirror, half expecting Dave Fever's body to stumble out after them like every zombie movie he'd ever watched. But no body, alive or otherwise, came outside, and soon the light from the Memorial Hospital was replaced with the interstate lights.

Neither spoke until Emily finally said, "Soooo…that wasn't normal?"

"Uh nope. That, um. That was something new." Shane's heart still pounded, the voice on a repeat track in his head. "I'll be honest, kid. I have no idea what that was."

"I'll tell you what it sounded like on my end," Emily said, turning her body towards Shane in the car. "One. Maria definitely killed him. No one says "that bitch" about a man, and you said so yourself that the angry detective didn't have any other female suspects." She counted the rest on her fingers. "Number two, Dave Fever was taken over by someone *not* Dave Fever to give us a warning about more murders. And number three, Maria is about to go on a murdering spree and kill two more people. Now the only question is how do we stop her without her killing one of us?"

"Well I have a lot more questions than that," Shane said.

"Oh right," Emily replied. "Who was the voice? Of course."

"No, kid. Not where my head was." He thought about Maria's odd behavior the day before in Mama Cate's. *She certainly is acting guilty. But why would she agree for me, and my TV crew, to look through the evidence if she murdered him? Maybe she knows who the murderer is and is afraid to come forward? But to Emily's point…who took over Dave's body?*

He shook his head. "We can't be sure it was Maria. And the voice just said 'Two more deaths.' That doesn't mean there will be two more deaths here, let alone two more murders by Maria." Shane drummed his fingers on the steering wheel, trying to convince himself of that last statement even as he said it. "And anyway... why would she want to kill Dave to begin with?"

"Did you see that guy? Dave looked like the kind of guy happy to punch his wife in the face. I don't blame her for murdering him."

"Can we not? We already talk to dead people, kid. We can't go around thinking murder is no big deal."

Emily snorted, folding her arms at her chest. "Cheaper than a divorce."

"You are never getting married if that's your rationale."

She waved him off, silent for the moment. "What if we Raise Dave again?"

"You want to bring Poltergeist back? No. First, someone is bound to see Dave's body by now so there will already be too many questions about what looks like a satanic ritual. And I don't even know if it's possible to Raise someone twice." He shook his head again. "No kid. No matter what happens, Dave needs to stay dead."

"Then it's good ole' fashion detective work to prove it was Maria before she can strike again," Emily said, rather too giddy given what she'd seen that night. "Let's go to her house."

"Oooh, hard pass. Confronting a potential murderess at night with my kid when I know zero self defense? No, we're going home. We're not telling my Dad what happened, and I'll come up with a game plan tomorrow."

"You mean 'we'," Emily said. "*We* will come up with a

game plan. I'm here. If I can learn to Raise the dead, I can help you solve an easy murder mystery."

Shane knew Emily meant gathering a plan to solve Dave Fever's murder. But the only plan he intended to make was how to get out of this case and out of this town as fast as possible. The Eastern European voice from LA popped back in his head, "*Don't go far, Bravo. We'll need you again soon.*"

We leave tomorrow, Shane thought as he turned the heat as high as it would go. The chills stuck to his body regardless. He drove as fast as possible away from Dave Fever's body and the threat of more murder to come.

5

Dead Guy at the Pump

MARIA DISCOVERED NOT LONG after moving to Hinnewatcha that getting gas was her favorite errand only because of the drive. Aster Lane weaved through the biggest trees in town, their fire tinged leaves stretching out across the narrow road as if to high five the branches on the opposite side. Hand painted signs along the way pointed to the smaller roads snaking off Aster, guiding tourists to apple farms and corn field mazes, and the morning sunlight dappled over the giant pumpkin farm sign at the last bend. Maria rarely filled up her tank more than halfway in the fall so she could drive to Dan's Diesel twice as often.

But she regretted the errand this morning as soon as she pulled in.

The owner's grandson paced outside the gas station entrance, cell phone attached to his ear. Red and blue flashing lights bounced off the pumps as a cop began to unwind yellow caution tape around a box truck parked on the far side of the gas station near the dumpster and the trailhead entrance.

Not here for you, Maria reassured herself as the lights flashed. She fumbled with the nozzle, nerves fraying, and willed the slow click of numbers to begin on the ancient pump. Danny put his phone in his pocket and chewed his fingernails in earnest as Maria walked up.

"Hey Danny, everything ok?"

He shook his spiky hair, his collection of piercings catching the flashing lights. "No, Mrs. Fever. I came in this morning and didn't think anything of the truck parked over there. But when I took out the trash it looked like someone was sleeping on the steering wheel. I went closer to wake him up, but," Danny folded his arms tight over himself, shaking his head. "But, um, he wasn't asleep."

"Dead?" Maria asked, stomach dropping. "Who is it?"

Danny didn't respond right away, he just chewed a bit more on the corner of his nail and eyed the truck. She was about to ask him again when he shivered and said, "Mrs. Fever, his throat was cut."

Maria took an involuntary step backward, "Jesus. Who is it?"

Danny just shrugged. "I don't think he's from here. I don't recognize him and the tags are from Massachusetts."

"Do you want me to call your dad?" Maria preferred to flee as fast as possible but she always liked Danny and his family. And the kid looked ready to faint.

"My parents are on their way." He looked past her at a car pulling up. "Never thought I'd be happy to see Officer Grumps."

Maria's reply was automatic, "Police Chief, now. And Levi's a good man."

"You can be an asshole and still a good person," Danny said, "Sorry. I need to get coffee if I'm going to get grilled by him now." He walked back into the building as Levi got out of his car.

He wore form fitted joggers and a lightweight sweatshirt as if he'd come straight from the gym. Regardless of what everyone else thought of him, you couldn't deny he was a looker. He glanced at Maria, his eyes dark under a furrowed brow, and said something to the other officer before making his way to her.

"Maria, I'd say nice to see you, but I'm assuming Danny already told you what happened," he said in lieu of a hello.

"Yea, awful." She shivered. Maria had to reign in vomit even just thinking about blood. "Do you know who he is?"

Levi shook his head, "Not local. It looks like he was just passing through. I don't need to tell you though that two murders in our town will be——-" He trailed off, cursing under his breath.

She turned in time to see a cameraman jump out of a van close to the yellow caution tape. The van had *Dead Don't Lie* and *Wednesdays 8pm EST* scrawled under Shane Bolles' face.

"You've got to be kidding me," Levi nodded once at Maria as he headed toward the van. "Best go on, Maria."

By the time Levi reached the other side of the small lot, another crewman was hoisting a boom mic over the yellow tape. Maria waited a few more moments, morbid curiosity warring with the need to get away, before she hopped back in her car.

***

Shane sat at his wheel in disbelief. He was almost to Hinnewatcha's lone gas station when he got the text from Frankie.

Another murder. Some place called Dan's Diesel. Crew already en route.

His plan to fill up before he told Emily they had to leave town dissipated when he spotted a familiar, attractive Latina woman hovering by the pumps. *What's the chance Maria is at two separate murders in a town that's seen zero murders in 50 plus years?* The not-Dave's warning from the night before rang out in his ears. *Two more deaths.*

Maria looked around her as if checking that she were alone, prompting Shane to drop any plan of leaving town just yet. He waited for her car to pass his before trailing hers.

She drove the final stretch of Hinnewatcha's most scenic road a solid 15 mph too fast, which felt like flying on these sleepy curves. Shane let his car fall further behind so she wouldn't realize she had a tail and dialed Frankie.

"Why are you driving away from the gas station?" Frankie asked, incredulous.

It was 5 a.m. in LA, but as always, the New York transplant sounded far too loud.

"How do you know where I am?"

Frankie huffed, "I track your phone since you always lose it, remember?"

"Uh no, don't remember that. It's creepy, but

appreciated." Shane put his blinker on when he saw Maria turn up ahead. "I was almost to the scene when I saw something suspicious."

"Tell me."

"It's probably nothing," Shane lied. Frankie was like a dog on a bone when he wanted to know something, but he didn't want the crew to follow Maria. At least not yet. He changed the subject, "How did you hear about the murder so fast?"

"Gary's got a police scanner in his room. He texted me on the way."

Shane pictured the heavyset cameraman hovering over an old-school radio, chain smoking as always. They'd never operated on a live case... everything before had been cold cases they'd meticulously researched for weeks before pursuing. "Why does Gary have a scanner?"

"He used to chase car crashes for KTLA, said the scanner is like white noise for him so he sleeps with it. Now tell me why you're moving away from a scene that will get 10,000 views before breakfast?"

Shane parked a few spots away from Maria in town, and took a quick glance at his hair in the rear view mirror while the DDL social accounts loaded. Sure enough, the 10-second clip of flashing lights and caution tape was getting more shares every moment. Likely because of the blinking text scrawled across the video feed.

Serial Killer Stalks New England Town.

"'Serial killer' is a stretch even for you," Shane said. Maria remained in her car, but he could see her mouth moving as if she, too, were on a call. "I told you yesterday that Dave Fever looked like an overdose."

"And, I sent you a copy of the toxicology report. An addict like that would have something in his blood. There weren't enough drugs, fun or prescribed, to have killed him." Shane heard the match light before Frankie took a drag of his morning cigarette. "You need to follow the wife. She's the main suspect according to the local cops."

"I don't think so. She seems chummy with the detective on her case, and I saw them interact. He was prepared to stamp it as an overdose."

"Is she as pretty as her picture?"

Shane bristled, not knowing why Frankie's statement made him want to keep Maria further from the camera. "She's pretty in a wholesome way. Definitely not your type."

"No shit, Sherlock. But she's probably pretty enough for a small town cop. I'd keep her out of jail too, if my only options were a bunch of churchgoers whose favorite high came from hiking or Bible thumping."

"I can't tell if you're serious," Shane said.

"I've never been to Vermont, but that's what I assume the dating pool is. Anyway, it's always the wife. I'll see what I can find out about the trucker and—" Frankie's quick inhale made Shane stop midway out of the car.

"What?"

"Holy mother of Bravo. Gary just texted me. She slit the guy's throat."

Shane slumped back down in his seat, tracking Maria as she walked across the town square ahead of him towards the library. Hinnewatcha's most notorious crime was from a car chase that happened back in the 60's. A gruesome murder would upend this town. He sent his dad and Emily a group text while he worked out what to do next.

Murder at Dan's Diesel. Meet me at home.

Frankie was typing something in the background. "Did you hear me Shane? I don't care what you're doing, get in front of the cameras. That place is about to blow up with reporters. Oh my god and it's just before Halloween. This is perfect."

Shane couldn't even respond before Frankie hung up on him. The pair had worked together for years, making a killing off of their reality TV show, but he had grown more obnoxious over time. Or maybe Shane was just as obnoxious and the incident earlier this year changed his perspective.

He debated in his car if he should turn around and trail Maria later when Emily's text came through:

At the library. I'll explain later.

He started to run before he realized people were staring. *No need to run. It's not like she's about to murder someone in the library at 8 a.m.* He slowed his pace a fraction till he got to the small corner library, using his long strides to make gains. Fat pumpkins clustered outside the door, and someone had hung a paper mache broomstick on the glass. The bell tinged, and three pairs of eyes turned to him in the small space.

Emily shared a table with a girl, maybe 7 or 8 years old. Maria had her hand on the girl's head and a stack of Harry Potter books laid in between Emily and the girl. *Has to be the daughter.* Their similarity was undeniable, and his own daughter's guilty smile was far too obvious. She waved him in.

"Dad! Come meet my new friend, Isa."

Maria looked ready to faint. "Isa honey, how did you meet Mr. Bolles' daughter?"

Isa bounced a bit more in her seat, "She likes Harry Potter, too! She said the first movie is playing at the Village Viewer tonight. Can I go?"

"Ah, I think it would be too scary, remember?" Maria said, glancing once at the door behind Shane. She white-knuckled her purse but released her grip when she caught Shane's eyes.

Emily piped in, her voice taking on a pep he hadn't ever heard. "I could take her if you want, Mrs. Fever. I know that movie by heart so I can tell her when to close her eyes. My name is Emily by the way, we met earlier outside of Mama Cates?"

Maria said, "Uh-huh, Isa, I don't—" at the same time as Shane said, "Not tonight."

Both kids paused, but Shane knew the look on Emily's face. Retreat was not in her vocabulary. "No seriously, Buttercup." He didn't want to freak either girl out, but he had to get Emily away from Maria. "Something happened with work and I need to take you home to Pops." *Hell, do I need to get both kids away?*

Emily snorted, but mercifully, didn't push as she stood up. "It's ok, Isa. This is my number. If your mom is cool with it, I'll take you some other time. We're here for at least a couple weeks."

Shane watched Maria as she crouched down to be eye

level with Isa. She pushed back a stray lock of the girl's hair and said something that made Isa laugh. Shane let go of a tension he didn't realize he held as he ruled out the possibility of her hurting any kid, let alone her own. He was distracted by his thoughts, though, as the door behind them pinged again.

Maria's face went pale. Shane turned around to see a lanky man with tattoos down his face walk through the door. He wore a gray and black flannel shirt that seemed to envelope his entire wiry frame. Shane glanced back at Maria and found her standing in front of Isa. He knew the protective stance of a parent, and regardless of what he thought her involvement was, he could also tell she was scared. He spoke before dwelling further. "Why don't Emily and I walk you guys home?"

Maria took her eyes off the newcomer for a split second. "I drove. But I'd love for you to walk us to our car."

The stranger scooted past them to the back shelves, as if oblivious to anyone else in the tiny room. Shane had never seen him before, but he spooked Maria. *She knows something,* he thought, as he held the library door open.

The girls chatted away ahead of them on the sidewalk, bikes in hand, when Maria spoke low to Shane outside. "Did you hear the news, then?"

He bobbed his head in a nod and put his hands in his pockets. "My crew heard it early this morning. Did you know the man that was killed?"

She shook her head, her thick dark waves bouncing even after she stopped moving. She turned to him, pausing their steps further from the girls. "I need to know. Am I a suspect?

I didn't even know what happened to that guy till this morning." Maria held herself and said every word faster than the last. "I just needed to get gas and I saw what happened. My mother is home, she can vouch for where I was last night and this morning. I've never even seen—"

Either she was the best actress, or she was freaked out in earnest.

Shane held up his hand so she wouldn't feel the need to explain further. He lowered his voice when her eyes began to water. "Honestly? It's not a great look. But I think I can help you."

"Why? You don't even know me."

"I don't think you slit anyone's throat," Shane said, surprising himself when he realized he meant it.

Maria glanced at the pair of daughters up ahead and whispered, "I don't want Isa to hear. She's had enough in her life to be scared of."

Shane touched Maria's arm, slowing them to a stop again. Emily glanced behind her and steered Isa towards the wooden playground further ahead.

"Did you know that man in the library?" He asked.

"No," Maria said. "He just feels off."

The hair on Shane's neck stood at attention. He'd never met anyone with any other abilities like his family, but he couldn't rule out the potential of someone else having 'freaky-weirdness' as Emily described their talent. "How so?"

"I don't know. I just get the creeps when he's around. Call it a woman's intuition."

"Have you ever spoken to him?"

She shook her head. "No. The first time I saw him was

when I pulled you and Levi to the back of Mama Cate's." She wrapped her mustard yellow cardigan tighter around her and the smell of cloves and cinnamon embraced him. Maria watched Emily push Isa on the swings ahead of them. "Your daughter is kind to play with Isa."

"Emily is great with little kids," Shane said, remembering how she devoured every Baby-Sitter's Club Book when she first found them. "She used to want to be a teacher."

"And now?" Maria asked.

He wasn't sure how they detoured off the problem at hand, but he didn't mind the break. "She says she's going to be a trial lawyer."

Maria barked a laugh better suited to a much larger man than such a short woman. She covered her mouth. "I'm sorry. I've just never met a preteen intent on being something other than a fashion designer or an astronaut."

"Eh, her mother was a designer. I'm pretty sure Emily would do anything so long as it's the polar opposite of her mother." *Why did you just say that? She's a suspect,* Shane thought, even as his own intuition said she wasn't.

Maria's eyes softened, so he turned away. He continued, "Anyway, she's good at grilling folks. She's a pistol to parent, but I know she won't put up with anyone's B.S."

Isa called over to them, "Mama, Emily said she'd help me bake cookies. Can she come over?"

Shane needed to get Emily home. There was no way the snoop was interested in baking cookies. And by the constant pings on his phone in his pocket he knew Frankie would blow a gasket if he wasn't in front of the camera soon. But for some reason, he wanted to keep talking to Maria. So, he just shrugged when she looked at him and said, "I'm an excellent cookie eater."

Maria pursed her lips, clearly not loving the pleas from the girls and zero back up from Shane. "Fine." She gestured to her car, "That's ours and we're just a couple blocks away. Follow us?"

"Love to." Shane watched the girls jump with excitement, even as Emily avoided his eye contact. He helped Isa wheel her bike to Maria's car, but when he went to pop the trunk, Maria blocked him.

"Nope! Can't fit in the trunk. I have a load of spices back there."

Shane could feel Emily's eyes drilling a hole in the back of his head. He relinquished the bike and let Maria shove it in the backseat. "See you in a few, then."

Emily spoke even before she buckled her seatbelt a moment later. "Murder weapon is in the trunk, then. You distract her, and I'll get the keys."

Shane wasn't sure how to respond. He kept alternating between Suspect and Victim every time he was around Maria. As much as he wanted to get out of Hinnewatcha, that nagging lure of nailing a case was hard to ignore. All of his cases were chosen because they were pretty much solved before they started filming. This could be his first, legit, case. But the feel of a bag over his head was a hard memory to shake. "We leave regardless of what we discover, or don't discover, in 30 minutes. Understood?"

Emily rubbed her hands together with glee. "This is so exciting. What happened this morning?"

"Another murder, kiddo. A bad one." Shane didn't

want to lie to Emily, and he needed her to slow down. Maybe a dose of reality would sober her up.

It had the opposite effect.

"That explains why she burst into the library. You flirt, I'll find the keys."

6

Cookies With A Murderess

Maria's white cottage nestled into her garden like a kitten ready to pounce. Orange and burgundy flowers brushed the low wooden fence, and fallen leaves rustled when Shane pushed the gate open. A low slung roof crouched over the front porch, and a knit blanket lay discarded over the wide swing at its furthest edge. Maria chatted with the girls as she unlocked her front door, and Shane noticed an open book next to a teal mug on the side table by the swing. He took a moment to read the spine when Maria was turned. *You are Only Just Beginning.*

Do murderesses get self help books? Shane shuffled his shoes on the pumpkin-shaped welcome mat before joining the others. The inside was like stepping into well-loved slippers. The cozy heat of the tiny fireplace embraced them, and the walls felt snug rather than small. A spice Shane couldn't name wafted from the kitchen a few feet away, and an older woman in sky-high heels craned her neck out from the doorway, eyes wide at Shane. He gave an awkward wave. *Too much elbow and no wrist,* Emily once pointed out in all her helpful preteen horror.

Maria and the woman whispered in Spanish together, too faint and too fast to even try to understand. Isa smiled apologetically at the Bolles and said a touch too loud, "Anyone want something to drink?"

The whispering ceased, and the older woman shooed Maria out ahead of her. "My name is Rosa Cruz, I'm Maria's mama." She gripped the sides of Shane's head and yanked him down towards her so she could peck either side of his face. "Now I understand you are the famous TV detective we've heard so much about, si?"

"Mama, enough." Maria gestured to Emily who was scanning every inch of the house without even trying to be discreet. "This is Emily Bolles, Isa's new friend, and her father, Shane Bolles. Isa wanted to bake cookies and Emily is kind enough to help. Isn't that nice?"

Rosa made a sound somewhere between a snort and a harrumph before crossing her arms. *Emily will have her hands full if she thinks I can just slip out.* Shane gave his best smile. "It's wonderful to meet you. Do you live here as well?"

Maria answered a quick 'no,' as her mother nodded an emphatic, 'yes,'. The older woman stepped ahead of Maria, taking Shane's arm and steering him further into the kitchen and away from Maria. "I do. Someone had to come take care of my poor daughter. She's been so distraught, barely eating in all her grief."

Shane watched Maria shove a fist-sized muffin into her mouth behind Rosa, as her mother continued. "We are so eternally grateful that you would come here and help us resolve Dave's case. The back and forth has been terrible for all of us, especially poor, poor Isa."

"Mama, please—" Maria interrupted as the girls weaved around them to pull out sugar and flour. The kitchen was not built to encourage a large gathering, and Shane's 6ft 4 frame came dangerously close to scraping the small white chandelier above them. Maria continued, "Why don't you help the girls with the cookies while Mr. Bolles and I have coffee outside?"

She grabbed the pot off the burner and two mugs before her mother could object. Shane silently groaned when he overheard Emily ask where the bathroom was, knowing every ounce of her time would be spent snooping.

Maria led them to two wicker chairs nestled into an overzealous garden. The coffee pot gave a hiss when it touched the stone table, but she didn't seem to notice as she handed him a cup of black coffee. "I'm sorry about my mom. She's a lot."

Shane waved her off. "No need to apologize, she's great. Reminds me of my mom."

"How so?" Maria asked, taking a sip from her own *Coffee or Death* mug.

Shane blew out a puff of air, wondering why he even brought his mother up. "My mom was a spitfire. She came up to maybe my chest but could make you feel about an inch tall if you ever talked back. But she was fiercely loyal. And she hugged hard."

"When did she pass?" At Shane's questioning look,

Maria continued, "You talk about her in past tense, I just assumed—"

"Right. No, sorry. You're right. She died several years back. This is actually my first trip home without her here." The mug in his hands was warm, and he felt a sense of deja vu from another garden a lifetime ago.

His mother ignored most flowers, but tended to her herb garden whenever the sun shined. She handed Shane an uprooted basil plant, the dirt warm from the summer sun. *"Deja vu, my boy, is someone on the other side nudging you to pay attention."*

He was distracted from the memory as Maria's warm hand closed over his own. "I'm sorry. That must be hard."

He blew out a breath. *OK, Mom. I'm looking.* He smiled, and despite the fact he had two murders to deal with, this moment felt right.

Maria's honey brown eyes were earnest as she said, "I love my mom. But, she's panicked about me and Isa. She always said we need a man." Maria pushed one shoulder back and let a Spanish accent thicken in an uncanny imitation of her mother. "A man will provide for you, and protect you, even from yourself."

Shane laughed. "That's a bit antiquated. Is your dad here as well then?"

Maria barked out her one syllable laugh, shaking her head. "Hell no. Mama has lots of advice for anyone within earshot, but it rarely applies to herself. After the divorce, she insisted no man would ever stay in her house for more than a night."

Shane asked, "So was she happy when you met Dave?"

She paused long enough looking down at her mug that he tried to take the question back. "I'm sorry, I didn't mean to—"

She waved him off. "It's fine. I just don't really know how much I can say without it going on your show or showing up all over the internet."

Shane blushed, chastened by her frank answer. He felt like a fluke sometimes, but never sleazy, and yet her answer made him realize what his show must look like to someone on the other side of his cases. He took a bracing sip of the black brew and said, "I understand." He looked around at the well-loved flowers spilling over pots surrounding them and the dead leaves beginning to pile up. The air smelled like brown butter and cinnamon thanks to the girls, and a neighbor burned firewood somewhere nearby. He scooted his wicker chair to be directly across from Maria and offered his mug up in toast. "As long as we are within your garden, anything you say will never leave this sacred space."

She laughed, clinking her mug to his. "Fair. OK. But if this is sacred space, then I need your assurance that if I spill my secrets, so will you."

"Deal."

***

Maria felt oddly relaxed given the fact that she was about to spill what could be damning evidence against her to a detective. But there was something earnest in Shane's face, and the way he talked about his own mother made her feel a little safer.

This will probably land me in jail.

She breathed out a cleansing sigh, ignoring that last

thought. "OK. When I met Dave, I was lost. Like literally and figuratively. I had just driven all the way from LA, stopping only to sleep for an hour at a time with Isa in the backseat. It was pouring down rain and I got turned around, but all I cared about was getting as far away from all the dead ends I'd found in LA I as fast as possible. I was out of money and looking for work when I pulled into the little garden center at the edge of town. And don't laugh," Maria pointed at Shane who innocently held up both hands for her to continue. "I swear, the rain stopped, the clouds parted, and the first person I saw was Dave."

Maria took another sip of the Columbian brew her mother liked best, picturing Dave and remembering the loamy smell of mulch. "He helped me. I told him I was looking for work, and he said that the garden shop wasn't hiring but he knew Mama Cate's was. And it felt like fate. I stumbled into this ridiculously adorable town like a wet, sleep deprived sea hag, and this stranger escorts me and Isa into a cozy bookstore-turned coffee shop—"

"—-turned wine bar and post office," Shane interjected, prompting her to laugh.

"Of course. Can't forget that." Maria continued, "And I got a job. Cate was there, gave me the keys to a vacant apartment she rented out, and told me I could start the following day. It was like a Hallmark movie."

Maria's heart still constricted when she thought about that moment. Even now it brought tears to her eyes that she willed back into her skull. She swallowed the lump in her throat. "Anyway. It's a small town, you know? I kept running into Dave everywhere. And despite some serious, flaming red flags, I felt like he was the reason Isa and I came here."

She scanned Shane's earnest face, lingering on his chiseled jawline a moment too long before she caught herself. She blew her not-bangs back again off her face, forcing herself to look somewhere other than his lips and pushed on. "So I caved to a date, even though I'd sworn off dating anyone else after the winners I'd left back in California. And then I said yes to another date, and ignored that warning bell in my head when Dave drank too much at dinner. And the next one when he kept cutting me off mid-sentence, or the fact that he kept a bottle of pills in his Carhartt that he never explained. And the dates somehow just snowballed. One day I was about to call things off and he surprised me by bringing me here, to this house." She gestured with her mug at the snug yard and flowerbeds surrounding them as if that was ever a good enough reason to stay. She grit her teeth, chiding herself for the thousandth time for not getting away from Dave sooner.

Shane didn't push her, didn't try to fill the gap that Maria left as she debated if she should continue. He just watched her with this intensity and, for the first time in years, Maria felt heard. She leaned back in her chair and he subconsciously mimicked her, his golden tan skin peeking out from his partially unbuttoned shirt. Maria pushed on, decided. "Every time I had one foot out the door, he had this big apology or a huge gesture that he'd change. He offered to see a therapist after the first time he hit me. That was two weeks after our wedding. And what do I do?"

Shane answered, without judgment or pity, "You believed him."

"Exactly. I believed his crocodile tears. And I made excuses when it happened again, or when he disappeared up to his brother's trailer for days on end. And somehow, the days sped into two years, and I—" *staged his overdose and poisoned his pills in the shed behind you.* Maria snorted, *Jesus, I am losing it.*

"—I, uh, was checked out. Mama wanted me to leave, to come to her in New York. She knew I was unhappy but didn't know the full extent of it. She just always said Dave felt wrong from the first moment she met him. But Isa was so happy, despite everything at home that I tried to hide. And I'll be honest, I love this town. I realize now that it was never Dave that brought me here. It was this place."

She leaned forward, the mug warm in her hands. "And because we're in this safe space, I'll tell you what's been weighing on me the most. I am not sad that he's dead. Dave was only getting worse with each day. And I don't know if I was going to be strong enough to leave him and this town, and this town felt like mine."

For a few moments the only sounds around them were of the girls chatting and shifting dishes or a car driving by in the distance. Despite the fact that she should have lied to him, Maria felt relieved. She hadn't been able to tell another soul what she just told this stranger. And that should freak her out, but for some reason, it didn't.

Shane leaned forward, putting his mug and then hers on the table before wrapping his large hands around hers. Every cell in Maria's body zeroed in on the electricity of his touch, and her pulse stuttered at the intensity of such a PG gesture. *Dios, what would it be like if he ran his hands elsewhere?* She couldn't pull her gaze away from him if she wanted to, and she would rather eat her right arm than look anywhere else. He appeared every bit the Hollywood Heartthrob, and Maria clamped her teeth shut so she wouldn't spew out the rest of her secrets.

"He sounds like a complete piece of shit."

Maria laughed, and tried to shift back to break the intensity but Shane gently pulled her towards him so the pair of them leaned closer, elbows on knees, hands in each others'. "I'm serious. He sounds like a complete jerk. And because we're in this safe space where anything you say will stay here, I'm going to tell you something. Self defense is not murder. And some people have a gray area of what is considered self defense."

The effect chilled all of the not-PG thoughts she had about this man, her muscles locking up in flight or fight mode as she dropped his hands. She leaned back, but he held his hand up before she could say anything further. "No, let me finish, love. If a man ever laid a hand on Emily, or tried to keep her down, I would help her bury the bones."

"I did not kill my husband," Maria lied, trying and failing to ignore the affectionate pet name. *Love. He's an actor, forget it.*

"I'm not saying you did. All I'm saying is that I don't care who killed Dave Fever. I'm just glad they did."

The screen door slammed, shocking Maria out of the safe bubble they'd formed around them in the mid-morning sun. Isa waved at them to come in, "Cookies!"

Maria's heart pounded, and Shane nodded to her as they

both stood. But when he squeezed her hand once as they walked to the house, she knew one sickening thought: *I want to tell Shane Bolles I killed Dave.*

7

Amateur Night

SHANE LET HIS THOUGHTS simmer as Emily talked without pausing on the car ride home. On the one hand, he wanted to leave town. The threat of multiple murders and the memory of that terrifying night back in LA screamed at him to get his daughter out of this town. *But where do we go?*

Beyond fleeing, he had a new, bigger problem at hand. All signs pointed to Maria as Dave's murderer, but more concerning than not caring, he wanted to help her. Every case he'd taken on since he learned how to Raise was to provide closure for a good family. To put the bad guy away. He had yet to pick up a case where he *liked* the murderer. He certainly never wanted to kiss a murderer before this, and it took every ounce of self control to not kiss her full lips in that garden and wash any thought of Dave Fever from her mind. He shook his head, forcing that thought out to focus on the issues at hand. *What do you do about the new dead guy?* Despite a lack of evidence, he knew in his bones Maria wouldn't kill a stranger. So now he had to find a way to shield Maria from Dave's case and find out who killed the trucker, both with rapid speed so he could get Emily to a TBD town since his location was all over social media.

"Are you even listening?" Emily asked.

Shane looked over at Emily as she brought him out of his brooding thoughts. Her pale blonde hair made the freckles across the bridge of her nose stand out more, a youthful contrast to the tiny piercing on one nostril. She was growing up too fast in LA. *One problem at a time.* "Sorry, Buttercup. Say again?"

An eye roll preceded her sigh, "I didn't see anything off in the house, but I also didn't get upstairs. How fast can you get to the new dead guy? Any chance you could take Maria somewhere so I can go back? Ooh! I could babysit Isa. Maria's pretty. Act like you like her and take her out to dinner and—"

"Slow your roll, jelly bean. We aren't snooping in Maria's house." Shane continued before Emily had a conniption. "I'm almost positive Maria killed Dave. She all but told me while you snooped."

Her mouth dropped open, comically agape. Then she asked, "Soooo why are you pulling into Father Time's house? Let's go to the cops."

"Because she did it to protect herself and Isa. Just like you called it. Dave Fever was hitting her, and though I don't know how she did it, she stopped him before he could do it again."

Emily looked at Shane, honest and open. He didn't push her; let her come to her own ideas, "And we're OK with that?"

"*I'm* OK with it. He was a terrible person. Maria is a good person. It isn't square with the law, but the law should have intervened before it got to this tipping point. The better question is, are you ok with it?"

She considered for all of a second, "Yep. Told you he looked like a wife-beater. So now what? What happened when I was at the library?"

They'd reached his dad's home again, Shane could hear the TV blaring from inside. "Let's go in. I'll need to fill Father Time in, too, so I'll explain it to both of you at the same time."

Shane had seen a lot of weird things. He saw his mother Raise dead people as a teenager and did the same thing for a Bravo TV show. He also lived in LA. But nothing could have prepared him for what he walked into. His father lounged in his favorite brown armchair in the living room with a bowl of popcorn in his lap watching The Real Housewives of Beverly Hills.

"Dad?" Shane asked, grinning.

His dad startled, spilling popcorn as he fumbled for the remote and turned it to football. "Jesus, Shane. I didn't see you! Are you trying to give me a heart attack?"

Shane pictured his dad lounging to RHOBH, raging at the TV, and couldn't help but laugh. "Don't change it on our behalf, we haven't seen that episode yet." He should let this go given how red Brandon Bolles' face was. He could feel Emily gearing up for the jugular next to him.

"It was a commercial. I was flipping through," Brandon tried.

Shane sat on the couch and he said before Emily could

say anything snarky, "That's fine. I can't stand Kyle anyway."

"You shut your mouth," Brandon retorted, then attempted to backtrack. "I mean, I'm sure she's a lovely person and doesn't need your critique. Not that I care. Or know who she is." He muted the TV. "Anyway. Where have you been? I got a call from Cate wanting to know if you're working on the new murder?"

"Probably," Shane said. "So I get a call from Frankie—"

Brandon interrupted, "You're still with that slimeball? I told you he was using you—"

"He's an agent, Dad. By definition he uses me. And just because he wears a few necklaces doesn't mean he's a slimeball."

His dad leaned back, arms crossed, and dismissed that argument for likely another time so Shane pressed on. "Anyhoo. I got a call from Frankie a couple hours ago to get to Dan's Diesel because a trucker with Massachusetts tags had been killed. I haven't been by yet, but apparently his throat was slit."

"And," Emily chimed in, far too cheery for the circumstance. "Maria all but confessed to Dave's murder because he was hitting her."

Shane cursed himself for not telling Emily to keep quiet. He needed a way to shield Maria from this before anyone else found out.

"Please tell me she's not going to do something stupid like turn herself in," Brandon said.

Shane blew out a relieved breath. He had a lot of issues with his dad left to resolve, but his brush over of Maria's murderer status let at least some of his guards down. He didn't realize how much he wanted his dad to be OK with his call to help Maria until he acknowledged her guilt aloud. "She didn't confess, but she looks ready to. Which is why we need to pivot and find out who murdered this trucker. I know she didn't do it, but if we can find who did, maybe the heat gets off Maria while we figure out how to help her."

"But here's another kink in the cog," Shane continued. "I don't think I can Raise the trucker. Something happened with Dave Fever's Raising." Shane glossed over the fact that Emily bore witness, but filled in his dad on what the Dave-turned-poltergeist said about multiple murders.

"So there's going to be another murder," Brandon mused after Shane finished. "OK. No, there's no way you can go back to Memorial Hospital after that fiasco. You're going to have to solve it old school."

Shane raked his hands through his hair, "I don't even know where to begin, Dad. I've only taken cases where I could Raise the dead. And even then we usually knew who was responsible before I took the case on. I could use some help."

Brandon cracked his knuckles, pulled out a notebook from underneath his chair and put a pair of reading glasses on. "I never thought you'd ask." He flipped past a few pages of scribbled notes. "All my findings pointed to Maria, though it's a shame that the toxicology report came out the way it did."

"You read the report in my file?" Shane asked, laughing.

"You left it on the kitchen table, so, yes. Obviously. Anyway, we'll figure out how to help Maria. Cate was hovering at the murder scene at the gas station. She texted me the license plate number. You can't talk to the dead guy, but you can still get access to everything that moody cop has. When are you going to the station?"

Emily piped in, fingers flying over her cell phone. "Looks like the sleuths are on it. Guy's name is Nathan Dass. Age 54. Lives outside of Boston. No kids, no wife. Trucker for Freight Folks."

Brandon leaned over to see the phone as well, mouth dropped open. "How did you do that?"

Shane groaned. He hated amateur detectives. They were like locusts, and they'd be all over this town by tomorrow afternoon. "This is going to turn into a circus real fast."

Emily was showing Brandon the TikTok videos of the social media sleuths. Brandon got up, "I need my laptop. And coffee. Want something to eat while you Tok?"

She just laughed. "No thanks. Dad, get out of here. We'll work on this end, you go talk to Chief Grump."

Shane followed his dad into the kitchen and said low so Emily wouldn't hear. "Dad, there's something else you should know." He knew he had to tell his dad what had been weighing on him for months. "A few months ago, I was kidnapped."

Brandon Bolles was his most terrifying self when he stilled. Like a predator ready to pounce. He just said, "I'm listening."

"I don't know how, but this gang leader knew what I could do. They threw me in the back of a van, covered my head with a bag, and made me raise a dead guy that was part of their crew to find out who murdered him. I didn't have a choice, so I did it, thinking they'd be done with me." Shane tried to ignore the rising nausea he felt thinking of that night. "They weren't. I get these phone calls every now and then. Not asking to do anything, but it's just his voice. Reminding me that they will need me again."

"That's why you came here."

Shane nodded. "There was a car parked outside my house last week. I can't be certain, but I had to get Emily out just in case. I didn't know where else to go."

"You did the right thing," Brandon said, arms crossed. "Did you tell the cops what happened?"

"No, they said they were watching me. They knew where Emily went to school."

Shane braced himself for the accusations that would be thrown his way. Hell, he blamed himself. Had he not done the *Dead Don't Lie* show no one would even know who he was. But Brandon didn't. He just nodded once, turned on the coffee pot, and said, "OK. Emily is safe with me."

Shane looked at his barrel chested father who gave him his own height. As a kid he always felt like his dad had hands the size of dinner plates, and even now as the old man gripped the half and half his beefy hands looked cartoonishly large. He believed him when he said he'd keep Emily safe, and some of the panic he'd lugged from LA dissipated. "Thank you."

He turned to go, grabbing his keys from the side table when his dad said, "I'll keep you safe, too, Shane. Let's just deal with one problem at a time."

Shane's throat clogged and he nodded once before leaving. He believed him.

***

Maria was grateful for the fact that Mama Cate's was bustling. It didn't give her time to dwell on the fact that she'd almost confessed to Shane Bolles the day before. She looked over at Cate's face, disbelief and confusion all over it.

"You want Matcha what?" Cate asked the annoyed college girl scrolling her phone across from the register.

"I got it, Cate. Swap."

Maria explained to the girl that they didn't have Matcha and talked her into a pumpkin spiced latte instead. Mama Cate's was sweltering despite the dip in temperatures overnight. She took off her heavy cardigan for a bit of relief as she rang up the next order. The line was out the door and there hadn't been a break in customers in hours. Outside, a cop directed traffic.

Cate groaned, and Maria looked up to see who had provoked her ire this time. Maria stifled a groan herself. Clarissa Baker, the town's mayor and real estate extraordinaire was sliding her way up to the front, cutting off annoyed customers. The woman was a walking opportunistic Karen. And she'd been all but giddy talking to the reporters out front all morning.

She waved her coffee mug at Maria, "I'll do another," she sing-songed before loud-whispering, "Less foam this time, though. It was like there was no espresso."

She jaunted off, waving at someone across the shop without paying. Again. Maria glanced over at Cate who appeared ready to chew her own teeth. Cate's husband Hamby actually relinquished his seat by the door to rub his wife's shoulders. Her boss was ready to murder anyone, and the last thing they needed was to make Clarissa, who also happened to be Mama Cate's landlord, mad.

"Get a bite to eat, Cate. I've got this." Maria said, and Hamby nodded his thanks to her.

"Wait," the lanky kid at the register said. "Aren't you that woman whose husband died?"

Maria needed to nip this in the bud before everyone else in the room heard. "What, because I'm Latina you think we all look alike?"

His face paled, "Ohmygod, no. Not at all. I would never think that, I'm so sorry. I just thought—"

"Right. You just thought." She clunked his Americano on the counter. "Your avocado toast will be a few."

He scampered off.

They'd stayed open an hour longer than usual, and Maria's feet ached by the time her shift was done. She locked up and took a moment to rearrange their pumpkin display that had become jostled in the line of customers that streamed through all day. Normally the town at night was quiet, peaceful. And yet, as she walked towards Town Hall she passed several people talking in front of cameras or their phones. The gas lit lamps were reinforced by bright Ring lights scattered throughout the town square. Every snippet she overheard prompted her to walk a bit faster.

"*—sleepy town faces double homicide in less than a month.*"

"*—the cops are quiet but the locals are not.*"

"*—with Halloween right around the corner, a serial killer—*"

She thought she'd be safe by the time she reached the

town meeting, but the crush of a crowd outside dashed that pipe dream. Maria shouldered her way through iPhones held aloft and spotted her mother and Isa with an open seat in between them.

"This is crazy, mom!" Isa said with a quick hug.

Her mother harrumphed next to her, but blessedly didn't add anything. "It's something, kid," Maria responded.

She glanced around the animated crowd. Almost everyone from Hinnewatcha was here. She spotted Shane and his daughter with a man she recognized, but didn't know, near the front. She tried to un-notice the way Shane's button down stretched over his broad shoulders. *Quit being a creep,* she thought as she forced her eyes away from his back. Cate and Hamby sat with arms crossed in the aisle behind them, but so many of the other faces were new. Officers walked around the room, and someone argued with Shirley in her uniform even as she shut the front doors.

Levi walked to the podium on stage. He wore his badge on his hip, his button down and tie in perfect order.

Rosa whispered, "You should bring that police chief some of your tea, Maria. He's so handsome."

Maria shushed her before she could say something more mortifying. Levi motioned for the crowd to quiet down, and for a moment the only noise came from the press cameras up front.

"Thank you for coming on such short notice. I know we're all eager to get to the bottom of this. For those of you who don't know me, I'm Levi Madison, Police Chief of Hinnewatcha and the lead detective on this case. Our condolences go to the Dass family in Massachusetts, and we appreciate the open line of communication between Mr. Dass' hometown police station and ours."

"There is a lot we don't know, but the point of this Town Hall meeting is to tell you as much as we can without impeding our investigation. I want to remind everyone that Hinnewatcha is a safe, happy town." His perpetual scowl deepened as he scanned the crowd. "We intend to keep it that way."

"Ay dios mio, Maria. Why hasn't he come over?" Rosa loud-whispered to Maria as she fanned herself.

She snorted and shushed her, "Dave's been dead less than a month, Mama. I'm not thinking about my next date." *Liar,* she thought.

Her mother elbowed her, "Of course. But holding hands with the fancy TV detective is ok, no?"

Maria glanced around her and said low, "Enough, Mama. That's not what it looked like. Now hush, please, I can't hear."

Rosa sniffed and pursed her lips, but fortunately didn't say anything else.

"—and we are not disclosing any suspects at this time, but we do suspect foul play." Levi continued at the podium, raising his hands at the murmurs growing in intensity from the crowd. "I'll take questions now."

Shouts rose up around them, people stood up with their camera phones rolling to catch the next words. Levi pointed at a slim reporter up front in a suit.

"Thank you, Rebecca Davis here with KMVO," she said. "Are you assuming the same murderer that killed Nathan Dass also killed Dave Fever last month?"

Maria sunk lower into her seat, squeezing Isa's hand that found hers.

Levi frowned at the crowd, silencing the pent up urge in the room to shout out more questions. "We have not suspected foul play in Dave Fever's murder and are treating these as two separate cases."

"Liar!" Someone shouted from the back, and every iPhone and head turned to the front doors.

Dave's skinny brother Greg cupped his hands over his mouth, shaking off an officer's hand that tried to quiet him.

"My brother was murdered and this two bit cop can't seem to see that! Where's the real detective?"

"I am the Police Chief and the lead detec—"

Shouts for Shane Bolles cut Levi off. Maria bristled on Levi's behalf. He'd been loyal to this town since he took this position and was a misunderstood, but respected, officer until Dave's murder. *I did this,* Maria thought.

The chants for Shane Bolles turned gleeful, and Shane reached the podium within a few strides. His hair was still coiffed to perfection, and Maria thought for a moment about their time in the garden when that hair fell into his eyes as he listened to her. *Dios mio. I do need to get laid. Knock it off.*

Shane smiled wide, but his face turned serious as soon as the crowd quieted. "I am only here to help support Chief Madison's team when needed, and I can assure you, he has the situation well in hand. Now let's give him a bit of grace here and let him finish answering your questions."

He stepped down at Levi's quick nod, and Levi pointed

to another reporter from the side whose question Maria couldn't quite hear.

Levi replied, "Correct, we do not think a curfew is warranted at this time and business will continue as usual. Yes, Mr. Timble?"

The ancient local pharmacist stood up, "If we had banned AirBnBs and short term rentals when I first suggested it, this would never have happened. Too many people!"

"Here we go," Maria mumbled as half the crowd shouted encouragement and the other half groaned.

Clarissa Baker seized that opportunity to vault onto the stage. She took the microphone from Levi as she smiled her picturesque Miss Vermont smile that won her the state's crown decades ago. She tapped the mic and made a simpering smirk as she waited for the cries to die down.

"OK guys... Most of you know me, but for the new faces in town, I'm Clarissa Baker, Hinnewatcha's Mayor. I'm also the resident real estate expert, and as we've discussed, Mr. Timble, more people does not mean more crime." She clapped the syllables to emphasize her point. "In fact, I'd argue that having this many new, young, entrepreneurs and law abiding citizens in this room is a *good* thing. That's why I've turned the old Sheridan at the end of town into world-class AirBnBs. That's right! And I've temporarily adjusted the empty office building into six individual AirBnBs as well given how popular our small town is right now."

"You've got to be kidding me," Cate shouted from mid-crowd. She didn't stand and ignored her husband, likely trying to hush her. "Do you really think this meeting or time is the most appropriate for you to hawk your personal real estate?"

"Ouch!" Clarissa drawled out the word and put a hand over her heart in mock protest that had some of the crowd chuckling. "That's a bit harsh. I am just looking out for our community's best interests. Our lack of hospitality units are not in line with our needs, and I'm just making sure we can *safely* accommodate these law-abiding citizens that have come into town to help solve these cases... which will in turn, make our community more safe. And who knows? Maybe some of them will stay and need a house." She winked and pointed to someone in the crowd before continuing, "Besides, Cate. I didn't see you complaining about the newcomers when the line from your coffee shop went out the door this afternoon."

Maria whispered to her mother, "This is going to get brutal. I need to get out of here. Do you and Isa want to come?"

Isa shook her head back and forth, "No way mom. This is about to get good."

Rosa shrugged, and Maria kept her head down as she hurried out the side door. She didn't see the men standing outside until she hit one of them with the door. "Sorry, didn't see—"

She let her voice trail off as she registered that one of the men was Greg Fever and the other guy was the face-tattoo man her instincts told her to stay far away from.

8

A Hinnewatchan Burial Ritual

MARIA DEBATED IF SHE should just dash back inside. Both the stranger and Greg jumped when she burst through the door without warning.

"Sorry," she repeated. "Excuse me."

She opted to beeline for her car instead, hoping the panic she felt would ease once she got away from them. She'd only made it a block away from Town Hall when she heard Greg shout.

"Wait! Maria, hold up."

She turned around and waited by Hank's Tools for him to catch up to her.

"What, Greg? I'm cold and I want to go to bed. Can it wait?"

He bent over, elbows on his knees, and held his hand up to catch his breath. He spit a dark glob of what she assumed was dip before asking, "Why are you running?"

"Because it's dark. Someone was just murdered. And I'm cold. Why are you running to catch up with me?"

"Something weird is going on," he said.

"Yea I'd say so. Not every day we have someone dead at Dan's Diesel with their throat cut."

"And it happened two weeks after Dave."

Maybe it was because she was exhausted. Maybe it was because the entire town would walk out of Town Hall any minute, but she didn't cower in front of Dave's brother for the first time in her life. "Greg. For the last time, *no one* thinks it was murder except you. Now, if you have something you're not telling me or the police, you need to say it. Otherwise let's bury Dave—," she caught herself before she could say 'so we can move on', "—so he can have some peace."

"Hell no. Things aren't adding up," he said as a couple passed by. He pulled her into the hardware store's alcove and spoke quieter. "There's stuff you don't know about Dave. And you don't need, or want, to know. But I'm not even talking about that. Something really strange happened last night."

Maria all but fell over with relief that Dave could have been caught up in something shady. She assumed this whole time Greg suspected her; it never occurred to her that someone else would want her P.O.S. husband dead. She shouldn't have been surprised. "OK. I'm listening."

"I have to ask this," he looked nervous. "Where were you last night?"

She snorted. "At my house. With my daughter and my mother. Why? Do you really think I killed the trucker?"

"What? No. But you know my ex, Tina? The one with the killer rack that works at Memorial?"

Maria had no clue and didn't want to think about anyone sleeping with Greg. But she nodded so he'd wrap this up.

"Anyway. She told me that they came in this morning and some ritualistic shit happened to Dave's body last night."

Maria stilled. She thought back to the tattered red string her grandmother Lita put on her as a child to ward off evil spirits. She'd ditched the string around the time she started wearing eyeliner and trying to straighten her hair. "What do you mean, ritualistic?"

"Someone pulled his body out of the bag in the middle of the night and there was like, herbs and black salt and stuff all over his body." He scratched at a scab on his forearm as he spoke, etching red lines over the tattoo of a skeleton screaming. "I don't really know how to ask this so I'm just gonna ask. Was it you?"

"Me?" Maria could have laughed. "No. Definitely not. Why would you think that?"

He threw his hands up. "I don't know! I just wondered with you being Mexican and all, and having your side business with the spices and shit, that you did it. Like some sort of burial thing."

She might have felt sorry for him had he not been so horrible to her over the last two years. He always seemed to rile Dave up, spouting off about a woman's place, and accusing her and Isa of being freeloaders. He never once spoke to Isa, and she always got the creeps whenever he was around. The brothers spent more time with each other than anyone else. He had to have known Dave hit Maria, and yet he never stepped in.

This conversation and her cold nose were irritating enough without being accused of being a Satanic cult member. She paused before she replied to the idiot so she could school her emotions and not lose her temper. "I am a Mexican American, Greg. I sell teas and spices to Mama Cate's, but that does *not* mean I'm hanging around dead bodies at night under the moonlight doing Satanic rituals. Nor do I know of any Mexican tradition where that would be even remotely normal. So no. It wasn't me." She stopped short of calling him a moron. "Wait, is that why you were talking to that guy?"

He leaned into her face far enough that she took a step back. "You need to forget you saw me talking to him." She tried not to gag from the stench of tobacco on his rancid breath.

"Jesus. No problem. I just assumed because he looked hispanic that you thought—"

"That's your problem and everyone else's problem in this shitty town. You just thought wrong. Now I'm not going to say this again—forget you saw me talking to that guy."

She held her hands up, "Fine. Done. Anything else you want to accuse me of tonight?"

"No." He turned to walk away but then faced her again with his finger in her face.

"But stop pushing to bury Dave. It's weird that you're not as concerned about who killed him as I am." He walked away, leaving her in the darkened alcove.

Maria waited until she stopped shaking to walk the rest of the way to her car. Everything about the Fever brothers felt threatening. She thought she'd be done with them when she poisoned Dave's pills, but it was like she couldn't shake them.

She needed to tell someone about this conversation with Greg. Especially if it could dig up another potential suspect and get any suspicions off her. *What the hell happened last night with his body?* She unlocked her car door, glancing in the back out of habit before getting in. She adjusted the rear view mirror and froze.

The man with the face tattoos, the one Greg wanted her to forget, watched her from under a gas-lit lamp post across the square.

She locked the doors right away and texted the number Shane gave her the day before.

Can we meet? Need to tell you something.

***

Shane glanced down at his phone. The Town Hall meeting about Nathan Dass' murder had turned into a group griping session about taxes and too many people. Emily read Maria's text over his shoulder and whispered, "Go. Father Time promised burgers after this so we'll meet you at the house later."

Shane nodded and slid out of his aisle and out the door, a pep in his step at the prospect of seeing Maria. He never saw her in the crowd earlier, and he'd shoved that disappointment down, reassuring himself like a twelve year old that he could swing by Mama Cate's in the morning.

Within a few moments her clunker of a car pulled up outside of Town Hall. The old deputy, Shirley, watched with a scowl as he got in Maria's car.

"Well, that was something," he said with a smile once he folded himself into her old Honda.

She took off, glancing so much in her rearview mirror that he had to ask, "What's wrong?"

"The guy from the library yesterday, remember? "

Shane remembered how she put herself between the stranger and Isa. She had tracked him the whole time with her eyes as they spoke. He nodded for her to continue.

"I think he's been following me. I've seen him all over this town ever since he got here, and then the library. No tourist ever goes in that library. And tonight, I ran into him and Greg arguing while everyone else was in the Town Hall."

"Look, I get that the guy is a little intimidating looking. But this is a small town—"

"I'm serious. He watched me talk to Greg after I left the meeting, and then he was lurking near a lamp post, watching me when I got into my car. That's when I texted you."

Shane swallowed the smile he wanted to grin when he realized she called him when she got scared. *Murderer,* he reminded himself. It didn't work.

"Hold up. What did Greg talk to you about?" Greg cornered him multiple times about Dave Fever's murder. He never outright accused Maria, but he wouldn't be surprised if he was a hair away from considering it.

"Oh, and that! That's the other thing. Greg said

someone was messing with Dave's body in the morgue? Apparently someone put salt and herbs all over his body. Do you have any idea what happened?"

Oh you know... my 14-year old and I Raised your dead husband and he all but confirmed you killed him before some other creepy spirit took over his channel to warn us that there are a couple more murders in our future. He said instead, "Nope. But Chief Madison mentioned that he had to go to Memorial in our meeting, I bet that's why."

Maria pulled off onto a narrow dirt road that snaked in between corn fields. It had been a wet summer, so the cornstalks were still drying down before the harvest. She parked her car on the side of the road, sandwiched in between dry yellow stalks of corn. Without saying anything else, she turned off the car and stepped out to sit on the hood. Shane looked around, but didn't see any cars or any lights for that matter in either direction.

The smell hit him as soon as he opened his door. He'd grown up around his parents' fields, but it was the corn mazes that came to mind before anything else at the musky smell of late harvest. He joined her on the still-warm hood of her car. Maria didn't say anything, but leaned back on the windshield with her arms behind her head.

The moon wasn't full yet but it was a cloudless night, and bright enough that he could see her face and the small puffs her breath made in the cooling air. He leaned back as well, hands stuffed inside his pullover. He was content to just lie next to her, even if she never explained why they were here.

She spoke after a quiet minute. "I used to come out here

when Dave was particularly nasty. I'd send Isa to my neighbors' house so she wouldn't see it, and on the worst nights they'd let her spend the night without me having to ask. If the shouting was loud enough, they'd text and say Isa was having so much fun that they wanted to know if she could stay. Offered a bed for me as well." Maria laughed, but he realized it lacked its normal punch. She wiped the back of her hand over her eyes, so he kept his gaze on the stars above. She continued, "It's Cindy and Eveline. Know them? They used to own the diner before they sold it last year."

"Oh I know them," Shane smiled. "Do they still keep a pack of French bulldogs with them at all times?"

"Yes!" Maria exclaimed, and he was grateful at the laugh returning to her voice. "They're always dressing them up in ridiculous outfits. It's why Isa wants to learn to sew... so she can give Puddles and Pickles new sweaters."

He angled his head so he could watch her profile as he spoke. "Cindy was my mom's good friend. They used to pair up in Bridge and just crow whenever they won. I thought Cindy and Eveline might break up after one particular drawn-out game."

Her full lips quirked up on one side. "I can see that. They're competitive as hell with each other. But loyal to the bone." She quieted for a few moments, and Shane relaxed further despite the windshield wiper digging into his back.

When she spoke again, it was quieter. "I felt safe here. Like I could come hide among the corn and under the moon, and he'd never find me."

"He's never going to find you now," Shane said, shifting

his body a touch closer. "That stage, that part of your life. It's over. Don't let him haunt you."

"What haunts you?" Maria asked after a moment.

He thought back to LA and the scratchy bag over his head earlier that year. The blinding light that swung above him when the bag came off, like a D-list Godfather. And he thought of the men in the shadows watching him, the lone light coming from the red tip of someone's cigarette. Maria nudged him with her shoulder, and he answered with more truth than he admitted to himself, "Bad men. The living ones. You'd think with all the dead people around me—the cold cases I mean— you'd assume it was the corpses that were the worst part of my job. But it never is."

"I guess it's a good thing you're really good at what you do then, right?" She asked.

He'd never felt like more of a fraud.

Yes, he did some good. He did some good to cases that were meticulously researched and ones he knew he could get an answer out of the victim. Sometimes they only took cases where the cops already had the proof, but the story of it would sell so they crowbarred their way into it. *What about the other hundreds of cases we've turned down?*

"It's a lot of show business," he said. "The real good comes from people like Chief Madison. He's kind of a jerk, but he is running a tight ship. And he cares. Probably too much."

"Levi's a good man. A lot of people just see the clipped answers and zero smiles, but he's definitely one of the good ones."

Shane wondered then if there was anything between the

two of them. On one hand, if Madison loved Maria, she wouldn't be on the suspect list for very long. He ignored the sting of jealousy he felt on the other hand. *You don't even know her. And you're not staying here.*

He asked, "Is there anyone in your past that would want to hurt you? A reason why the guy with the tattoos could be following you?"

"No," Maria shook her head side to side. "I dated a lot of jerks in California, but they were losers. Not guys that would want to come looking for me. Most are probably where I left them... high on a couch somewhere."

"What about Isa's dad?"

She laughed. "No. The only good thing that guy ever did was move back to Venezuela. He was gone months before Isa was even born, and we've had zero contact since the day I told him I was pregnant."

"I never understood men like that. Emily, in all her pre-teen angst, is literally half of me. And I'm amazing enough that I'd love to see another version of me play out."

Maria barked her laugh then, and sat up fully to face him. "What about her mom? Where is she?"

"Ugh. Leslie is apparently an Influencer now after years of trying to make it as a self-proclaimed fashion icon. She liked the red carpet and the parties and that was all great when I did, too. But then we had Emily, and leaving her night after night felt gross. By the time Emily was four, I'd already moved out. She didn't even fight me for full custody."

"Is she in Emily's life at all?"

"Only in phases when she remembers she's a mother.

She would ask to scoop Emily up to take her shopping, and I let her go thinking Emily needed that one-on-one time. And she did at first. God, it was like Emily was on cloud nine when she would get that phone call. But then something would come up, and Leslie would bail at the last minute, and it just crushed her."

"That's terrible," Maria said, rubbing her hands together and blowing some warmth into them.

"It was soul-crushing to watch. I'd do anything to make it better, and tried to keep her away from Leslie, but Emily pushed back so hard. She was mad at me, mad at her mother, mad at the world. She started to act up in school, ditched her friends, whole nine yards."

Maria asked, "Are you closer now?"

"A lot. She still pushes back on almost everything, and sometimes I feel like she's the parent. But she's a smart kid and got her act together before it took her too far down the wrong path. Now when Leslie calls she'll pick up just to hang up on her."

"Good for her. She seems like a sweet kid with Isa."

Shane felt guilty for the fact that Emily was not above using Isa to snoop. He was about to ask something else when Maria beat him to it. "Shane, did you really come here just for Dave's case?"

He shook his head and answered honestly, not quite dwelling on why he wanted to tell her the full story. "No. Emily and I needed a change of scenery. Dave was a weird coincidence that my agent and producer jumped on as soon as he heard."

She nodded without saying anything, but seemed to withdraw at that reminder. "Will you do me a favor?'

His answer was immediate, "Anything."

She climbed off her car and wiped her hands on her jeans. "Can you look into that guy with the face tats? Also Greg got cagey earlier and said a few things that made me think the two of them were doing something shady together. I know you're probably not allowed to tell me anything and I shouldn't—"

"I don't care about that. I'll let you know anything I find out."

She smiled then, and turned away from him as if to hide it. She craned her neck back, rubbing her hand over her collar bone as she looked at the sky above. Shane had the overwhelming urge to haul her back against the hood of the car when she said, "Looks like we could have a Moon Dog soon."

He froze, the Polgergist-Dave's warning clanging between his ears. *Two more deaths to come before the darkened moon meets the canine.* "What did you say?"

She already had her car door open and looked at him with her head cocked as he stood there rooted to the spot. "About the Moon Dog?"

"Yeah, what is that?"

She shrugged and waved her hand in the air as if his heart wasn't about to fall out of his chest. "I think it's actually called a parselene, but my grandmother Lita always called it a Moon Dog. It's when it looks like there are two bright spots—or eyes—on either side of the moon."

He hurried to the passenger side and got in. "And when does that happen?"

"It's rare, but if we have a clear sky and the clouds are wispy it can happen. Why?"

He couldn't hear over his own heartbeat. *It's not exact,* he tried to reassure himself. *The voice didn't say "murder" and "darkened moon meets the canine" could mean something else.* But each thought circled back to his panic that another murder, one closer to home, would occur.

No spirit ever hacked someone else's channel like it did during Dave's Raising. Neither he nor his dad ever heard his mother speak of anything similar. And out of the hundred or so dead he'd personally Raised in his life, no spirit ever felt something strong enough to hijack another's Raising to give a warning. *Was it to warn me about my family? Or did it hijack Dave because it thought I could stop it?*

He ran his hands over his clean shaven face. "So is this like a full moon when it's a Moon Dog, or a waxing whatever?"

Maria turned the car when he pointed to his dad's road and said, "Usually. If it's not a full moon, it's just after."

"Do you know when the next full moon is?"

She shrugged, "No clue. Google will, though."

"Right." he said, not hearing much else as he got lost in his own thoughts. *Find out when the next full moon is. Figure out who this guy is that's potentially stalking Maria. And stop a murder of someone you may care about that may or may not happen by a perpetrator you may or may not know.*

Great.

9

Tat Face or Face Tat?

Detective Levi Madison tugged at the tight tie at his throat on Maria's porch the next morning. Maria shouted through the wall that she'd be out in a moment while frantically shooing her mother out of the foyer.

"Mama, *please*—"

Rosa put her hands on her hips, refusing to budge. "Invite the man in, *mija*. It's not polite."

"It's also not polite to eavesdrop, and yet, you and I both know, you'll listen to anything we say from the other room," Maria hissed. "Where in the world did I put my coat?"

"I can't help it, you have a loud voice. It's like a boom," Rosa said, flashing her fingers out wide in imitation of a bomb. But she turned and slowly sauntered out of the room, heels clicking all the way to the back of the house.

Maria found a semi-clean sweater on the couch and threw it over her head. She walked out the door, still trying to disentangle her curls from the tag and smiled wide.

"Chief Madison! H-how are you?" Maria's head was still cocked sideways while her fingers searched for the snag.

He stood still, likely waiting for her to stop being a spaz, before shaking his head. He walked across the porch and disentangled the god-awful tag from her hair without a word. He didn't let go of the curl though right away, and Maria held her breath at his sudden proximity.

Up close she could see the slight salt and pepper stubble against his skin. It angled across his sharp cheekbones and Maria itched to trace that line with her fingers. He shifted her curls, like he was setting them to rights, and Maria's face heated. He finally made eye contact and dropped his hand.

His slight step back felt like a welcome gust of cool air, but he said, "Please, it's just Levi."

She nodded, and somehow found her voice over her pounding heart. "Then I'm just Maria."

He smiled, and she basked in that rare show of emotion. "What?" He asked.

Maria bit her lip, attempting to not look like a grinning idiot. "Sorry. I'm just not sure I've ever seen you smile." She stopped him before he could go back to scowling, "It's a good one. You should do it more often."

He ran a hand over the back of his close cropped hair and she thought for a moment that he blushed as well. But when he looked up he was back to the stone faced detective she knew. "Maria, I got a call from Shane Bolles. Why didn't you call me when you thought you were being followed?"

Maria didn't know why, but it didn't occur to her in her panic to call Levi last night. She only thought of Shane. "I don't know, to be honest. I didn't think I was being followed until last night when I was getting in my car. And besides, you were dealing with the Town Hall meeting."

He huffed out a laugh. "That was miserable. I would have skipped out of the building mid speech had you given me a reason. But in all—" he paused mid-sentence, looking over Maria's shoulder.

She glanced back to see two sets of eyes disappearing behind the curtain. "My mother is staying with us," she said by way of explanation. She glared at the curtains still swaying. "Want to take a walk?"

He held his arm out for her to walk first, and Maria thought back to all the times Dave walked five steps ahead of her. He constantly complained about how slow she and Isa walked. *Stop thinking about Dave,* she thought. She focused instead on the sidewalk ahead of them and the soft warmth of the autumn sun on the bright and cloudless morning. They ambled along, and she opted for the route that would wind them around the homes with the best gardens.

It was early enough that most people were still in their homes. Puffs of white smoke snaked out of stone chimneys, and the steady raking of leaves from a few yards over calmed her. It was hard to believe that bad things ever happened in this town at all. *And yet, you committed murder. You started this mess.*

They walked in amiable silence for almost a block before Maria realized she wasn't rushing to fill the void. She had never spent much time with Levi before. He'd gruffly said hellos and things of that nature around town, but even when he'd taken her information and alibi after Dave's body was found, they'd been surrounded by other people. She didn't know anything about him. Other than that he never wore a wedding ring and he didn't have kids at Isa's school.

"Maria, I've been looking further into Dave's death ever since the toxicology report came out."

And just like that, the easy contentment Maria felt walking by Levi's side whooshed out of her. Panic hunkered down in its place instead.

He continued: "Specifically, into who he was associated with prior to his death." He motioned for her to sit on the bench in the pocket park tucked in between two of Hinnewatcha's oldest homes, which suited her just fine. She was already nauseated from the highs and lows of this conversation.

"Do you know what Dave was doing for his brother before he died?" He asked.

Maria shook her head, "No. He would go up to Greg's house a few nights a week and come home drunk or loaded, but he never told me what they did." *Nor did I ever ask because it meant he left me alone for a while.*

"Have you ever found more pills than he would take himself in your home?"

"You think he was selling?" If she could kill Dave again, she would.

"I'm wondering if that was the intent. There's a rumor that one of the bigger drug runners in New England had a shipment stolen. It started a turf war that's made its way to Vermont. And according to the police in Albany, one of their insiders thinks some small-time dealers in our state are responsible."

Maria's head reeled from the implications. "So, are you

saying that someone could have killed Dave because he stole this kingpin's drugs? Is that why the trucker was killed?"

"I don't have enough to link the two. The two murders, if we're working on the assumption that Dave was murdered and didn't overdose, are completely different in nature. And I don't have any proof that the Fever brothers are the ones who stole the pills to begin with."

"Have you looked at Greg's place?"

He shook his head. "I'd need a warrant for that, and I don't have enough evidence for a judge to grant me one, at least not yet. That's why I need to start with Dave. Did he have any storage units or safes? Is there anywhere you can think of that he could have hidden a stockpile of drugs?"

She held her hands up, "I would never allow a stash of drugs like that in our home. Dave kept pills, but I never saw more than a bottle or so at a time, and he usually kept them on himself. I've got Isa, and I don't want anything threatening her. The syringe found next to him was the first I'd heard of him injecting anything."

He put his hand on her knee. It was for half a moment but it was soothing enough to calm her frantic heart at the implication. "I don't think you would. The Fever brothers have enough possession charges in their history that would make them suspects, but as far as I know, you have nothing in your history, correct?"

"Right. I've never even vaped. Drugs scared me, even as a kid running around LA with a bunch of other kids that had zero hesitations when it came to drugs."

"As they should."

"It wasn't really the drugs. It was Rosa Cruz. I can't

imagine what my mother would have done had I even been caught smoking a cigarette, and even though we weren't always close, just the thought of her reaction kept me away."

He laughed and leaned back against the bench. They watched a toddler scoot merrily past them on a small bike, his mother running after him. Levi sighed once and then said, "I've probably said more than I should. But I wanted to give you a heads up so you're not caught off guard. And I don't think this needs to be said, but stay away from Greg Fever. Even if he's not involved, he's no good."

"I'm aware. And I'm trying." Maria and Levi stood up and began walking back in the direction of her home. "Levi, I saw Greg talking with the guy with the face tattoos outside while everyone was in the Town Hall. Afterwards, Greg cornered me and told me about something that happened to Dave's body. What happened?"

"Officially? I'm not allowed to say anything. But unofficially, we have no idea who or why someone would do that to his body. It doesn't add up. The only thing I can think of is that it's some sort of Halloween prank or séance. We get enough crazy people visiting this town during this time of year because of Burial Rock."

Hamby told Maria not long after she moved to town about the Abenaki burial site. The mountains and rivers around Hinnewatcha were once home to the Western Abenaki tribe. Archeologists speculated that a group of rocks in the woods behind Dan's Diesel could have been an old burial ground for the tribe, but they couldn't prove it because locals had raided the place around the turn of the century. Ever since, a rumor persisted that on fall nights the ghost of an Abenaki woman stood over one of the rocks. She was called The Protector. A few B-list documentaries were made about it, but for the most part, it only became popular around Halloween when teens dared each other to camp out near the rocks.

Still, Maria thought, *taking a body out of a morgue is a ways away from camping near a haunted rock.* She packed away that thought to focus on something tangible.

"Greg thought I might have done it as a Mexican burial tradition."

"Greg is an idiot," Levi responded immediately.

She laughed at that and its simplicity. "Agreed. But when I brought up the fact that I saw him and the face tattoo guy talking, he got really defensive. Told me to forget I saw them together."

Levi didn't say anything right away. He processed it silently, as he seemed to do with most conversations. A few moments later he said, "Thank you for telling me that. After I got Shane's call this morning, I put one of my deputies on the newcomer's tail to keep tabs on him."

"Thank you," Maria said.

"Shane seemed worried about you," Levi said, looking down at his shoes once before turning back to her. "Did you know him before Dave's death?"

It felt like a probing question, but then again, he was a detective. "No, I just met him when he got to town. He seems like a nice man, despite all the cameras."

Levi nodded. "He's actually not as bad as I thought, but his crew is rather aggressive."

"How so?" Maria asked as they reached her front gate.

She was surprised her mother wasn't waiting on the front porch.

He waved it off, "It's nothing, I shouldn't have said anything." He put a hand on her forearm before she opened the picket fence. "Maria, I'd like to put an officer on night watch outside your home for a few days until we figure out who this newcomer is."

"That's really not necessary," she said, though part of her was relieved that someone else would have eyes on her home while her mother and Isa were there.

"Humor me. I'll sleep better knowing you're safe."

She smiled at that. "Thank you. And Levi?"

He turned around, hands in his pockets. "Yea?"

"If I find anything like we discussed, I'll call you first."

He smiled, a true second smile at that. "Thank you."

Maria turned, wondering how fast she could get her mother and Isa out of the house so she could dig up every inch of her home. If Dave hid a stash drugs in there, she'd find them.

***

Two hours later, sweaty and out of cuss words, Maria put down the hammer. She stopped short of ripping up floorboards. She scoured every inch of her home looking for a hidey hole Dave might have found and came up empty. She didn't find any notes or receipts indicating he had a storage space elsewhere, there were no obvious dug up places in the yard, and nothing abnormal about her potting shed.

She cursed him for the hundredth time and knelt down in her flower bed to work out her frustrations on the remaining chamomile flowers. Usually the act of harvesting the flowers would calm her, but even after small buds piled around her like confetti, she couldn't sit still. Her thoughts kept drifting back to how she got to this place in life.

Somehow the defiant, angry girl she'd been in New York had given way to a woman she was only just now getting to know. She'd let each disappointing relationship chip away at her on the other side of the country. Dave had taken advantage of her vulnerability by the time she came back to the East Coast, but she was the one that let him whittle away at her until only a hollow shell of herself remained. The girl her mother and aunts raised would never have let a man control her. Let alone hit her.

She attacked the flower bed, muttering to herself all the things Dave preached.

"Women should respect the man of the house."

"Women should know their place."

"Isa has a mouth on her. She'll learn."

She let the hot tears wash over her face, and welcomed the cramp in her hand from gripping the clippers.

"Divorce isn't a word in this house."

"No one will believe you."

"You'll leave over my dead body."

There are sentences that change lives forever. Small moments that to anyone else would be inconsequential but to someone listening, to someone paying attention, those moments would be earth shattering. That sentence came when she brought home an almond croissant from Mama Cate's for Dave one day.

"What kind of wife doesn't know her husband is allergic to almonds? Even just smelling those will send me to the hospital. Are you trying to kill me?"

She stood in the kitchen, rooted to the spot, when he stormed off indignant and raging. That tiny pastry cracked open her hollow shell, allowing the powerful force she once was to trickle out. She didn't decide to kill him then, that didn't happen until after the incident with Isa, but she began a mental list of things she might need if he ever had to go as she clutched that croissant. The list gave way to measurable steps to take her life back, and now she refused to go back to the woman that felt helpless.

With each snip of the flowerheads she listed and discarded any place she knew of that Dave could have hidden a cache of pills. She was left with only one conclusion: Anything Dave hid had to be at his brother's place in the woods. By the time she loaded the flower heads onto a drying rack, she had made her decision. She'd find whatever evidence she could so no one would ever realize that she was the murderer. Maria grabbed the jar of lavender and chamomile tea leaves she'd made the week before and hopped in her car.

***

"We gotta talk about the bigger problem," Brandon said as he snapped the lid of the dry erase marker back on.

Shane, Emily, and Brandon Bolles sat in front of the large whiteboard on wheels that Shane's dad purchased the day before. Notes and pictures of everything they could pull on the murdered trucker and their list of suspects were taped to the board, and the opposite side held ideas on how to cover Maria's tracks.

Shane looked over at his daughter on the couch, who at some point shoved a pen behind her ear, identical to how he stashed his pen. She threw her hands up, almost toppling her laptop out of her lap. "What have we *not* gone over? We've been at this for hours."

His dad replied, "We can't keep talking about the guy as "the guy with the face tattoos," or "tattoos on his face." It's too clunky. How do you not have a real name yet?" Brandon leveled the last question at Emily as if she was holding something back. She replied instantly, "I love how you just learned about the internet two days ago and suddenly have an issue with how fast I can find information on it."

Shane ignored their banter. It at least lacked the heat it did when they first arrived, which was a good sign. "I personally prefer Tat Face," he said, hand raised.

"You would," the other two replied simultaneously. Brandon wrote *Face Tat* instead above the suspect's photo.

Brandon, suddenly better suited as a general than a farmer, paced in front of the whiteboard. "Let's recap. We know the trucker, Nathan Dass, racked up significant gambling debt according to Shane's new buddy."

"I like Shirley," Shane mused. The old deputy loved a good gossip and had zero issues recapping everything Levi Madison's team was looking into.

"We also know that Face Tat had some sort of heated discussion with Greg Fever, which likely means they met prior to last night's Town Hall."

"I still think we need the mayor on here," Emily said as

she tapped her pencil against her laptop. "She's way too peppy for a murder to have just taken place in her town. I saw her waving a pack of TikTokers into her AirBnBs like she was a tour guide."

Brandon scoffed, "I'm pretty sure they're called Tikkers."

She looked at Shane, "I can't tell if he's serious."

"I think you need to get off the sleuth pages for a bit, kiddo. The conspiracy theories are going to your head," Shane replied.

"Hear me out," Emily said, taking the dry erase marker from Brandon. "First, she put an offer on all the land surrounding Dan's Diesel one month prior to the murder. The LLC she owns applied for a multi-family permit to build 250 townhomes on that land. And, ScoobyRoo sent,—"

Shane raised his hand again, "I'm sorry, what?"

"Right? 250 townhomes! And that's not—"

He shook his head. "No, no Buttercup. You're getting your facts from someone named ScoobyRoo?"

"He called the Mailman Murder before you did, and you had to Raise the mailman from the dead to get that confirmation. Even Frankie said the sleuth had talent," She replied, arms crossed.

"Frankie gets on those accounts just to stir up controversy so younger people will watch the show."

"And Frankie is a scoundrel," Brandon chimed in.

"Are we suddenly interviewing for the Renaissance Festival? Who says 'scoundrel'?" Emily said, relinquishing the dry erase marker back to Brandon. "We need to go back to the voice."

Shane shuddered and glanced over at his dad's hopeful face. "Dad, I know you want it to be mom, but there was nothing warm about the voice that spoke through Dave Fever." He pushed through the lump in his throat that always formed when he thought of his mom. "I think she is watching us and rooting for us, but whoever, or whatever, spoke wasn't Mom."

"I heard some kids in town talking about the Abenaki ghost in the woods behind Dan's Diesel," Emily said, chewing on the end of her pen. "They call her The Protector, and said she stayed behind even after her tribe moved away. Maybe she's protecting this place."

A knock at the front door interrupted their discussion, and Shane mulled over Emily's words while his dad got the door. A few moments later, Brandon said in a loud, dramatic voice, "Oh hello, Maria Fever! Please, come in!"

Shit. Emily and Shane sprang into action and gathered up every photo and note they had on the table. Emily pushed the whiteboard into Brandon's room just as Maria walked in the living room.

"Hi, I'm sorry. I didn't mean to interrupt," she said, holding a jar of something in her hands.

She looked disheveled, and Shane was pretty sure there was a dead flower trapped in her wild curls. Suddenly he realized why she might be here. *I should have asked her first.*

"Uh Dad, Emily, can you give us a few?"

His dad beamed. He'd met Maria briefly when she dropped Shane off the night before and she was now his new favorite Hinnewatchan. Brandon motioned for Emily. "Come on, hippie, I bet you'll like the Farmer's Market and it's still open for another hour. Let's let them have the house to themselves for a bit."

"Way to make it weird, Pops. Thanks." Shane said, avoiding Maria's face. When he got the nerve to glance over she was silently laughing behind her hands. He waited until he heard the front door shut and said, "I'm really sorry. He's lived alone for too long apparently."

"It's fine. He's great," she replied.

They spoke at the same time, "I'm sorry for not calling first—"

"I told Chief Madison what you said."

She laughed, and the nerves Shane was juggling lessened. He motioned for her to sit and said, "You go first."

"Thank you," she said, nestling back into the old leather couch. "It's fine. I would have told Levi at some point. I'm not sure why I felt like I should talk to you about it first."

"I'm glad you did, but I don't know how to protect you. I knew Madison could." Shane scooped up a note Emily scrawled about the Abenaki ghost on the coffee table and shoved it into his back pocket. "So, is that why you came by?"

"Not quite," Maria said, biting the corner of her lower lip. " I need a favor, but it's something I'm afraid you'll say no to."

"I doubt I could tell you no," he said before he could stop himself. She was fiddling with the ring on her right hand so he knew it must be bad, but he didn't care. He was running headfirst into the fact that making this woman happy made him happy. *Bad idea. You're not staying. And if she knew you were a fraud, she wouldn't give you the time of day.*

She clapped her hands once and the words rushed out. "OK. I need you to go with me to Greg Fever's property so we can look for a pile of drugs I think he and Dave stole."

"Wasn't expecting that," Shane deadpanned.

She stood up, pacing, and walked him through the conversation she had with Levi Madison earlier that morning. Ten minutes later, she'd convinced him despite every warning bell in his head.

He pointed her to the only bathroom on this floor when she asked, and he texted Frankie back while waiting on her. The run through with his cameraman yesterday wasn't his best, and Frankie was quick to tell him as much. He didn't care. He had yet to tell him that this would be his last show. Ever since Frankie became the main producer for *Dead Don't Lie* he'd become far more opinionated on everything Shane did on the show. *As if that man needed more opinions.*

He heard Maria wash her hands and looked up when she paused at the doorway. It was only then that he realized she was in his dad's room. With the whiteboard. He froze. *It might be on the trucker side.*

"Why do you have my picture taped up here?"

Not on the trucker side. He rushed in to get her away from reading the rest, but it was too late. She stepped back when he tried to touch her shoulder.

"You guys think I killed Dave?"

He probably should lie. But he needed her to know that he was trying to protect her, that she could trust him. "No. I know you killed Dave."

It was the wrong thing to say.

10

It's Just Show Business

MARIA BACKED UP AGAINST the doorway, out of Shane's reach. "I didn't kill Dave," she lied. "Don't touch me."

He held his hands up as if she was just a skittish animal that needed placating. "You don't understand. I don't care that you killed him."

"But I didn't," she retorted, looking around for another way out of this room.

"Let's just say you did," he blocked her exit from the bedroom. Shane was a tall man, and he looked larger than normal in the low ceiling of his father's house. Maria wasn't afraid of him, but she didn't want to be in this room with him a moment longer. She felt the bands of nausea crawling up her throat again. *Don't think of prison. Don't think of Isa. Stop thinking about prison and losing Isa.* Nothing helped. She needed to get outside.

"—all I would do is try to help you," he finished, but she only half heard him.

"Help me?" She laughed, "You? With the whiteboard and your dad, and *Jesus*, your daughter, too? You expect me to believe that if I murdered Dave, which I definitely didn't, you guys would help me?" Her racing heart constricted and no amount of self-help podcasts or lists would calm her now.

"I know you killed Dave, Maria," Shane said, blocking her way again when she tried to move past. "And you should have. He was a horrible person that exactly zero people—well maybe his methy brother, but no one else—will miss. And based on what you told me, it was only a matter of time before someone killed him. You just probably helped some kingpin by saving him the time and trip up here."

"So now I'm helping drug lords?" Maria asked, her voice pitching higher by the moment. *Get a grip, he needs to think you think he's an idiot. Stop acting guilty.*

"You know what I think?" She said, pushing her finger into his chest and forcing him to step back out of the doorway. "I think you're all smoke and mirrors. I think you're grasping at straws because you have no freaking idea who murdered Dave or this new guy and you need to pin it on someone because the cameras are rolling. Well it's not going to be me."

He flinched. It wasn't obvious, but she caught the movement regardless. Maria would have normally felt about as tall as an ant at hurting him, but she needed him to doubt his assumptions. And she had to get out of this house and into fresh air.

"Do not call me again," she said, retrieving her scarf from the couch. She stalked around the coffee table and stood as tall as her short frame allowed, punching out each syllable as she tried to tie her blanket-sized scarf around her neck. "I don't want to see you, or your kid, near my house. And I swear to Fall Jesus that I will call an attorney if I see *any* cameras near my home. Do you understand me?"

"Is there a Spring Jesus?" He asked, ignoring her threats. *Of course he would. I'm sure Bravo has a ridiculous amount of attorneys on call.*

"I'm serious, Shane Bolles. Stay the hell away from me and my family. I will tell you this only one more time. I. Did. Not. Murder. Dave."

He swore under his breath and turned away for a moment, rubbing his hands over his clean shaven face.

"Ohmygod, Maria. I know you killed him, and there's a good chance Levi Madison and the rest of this damn town know, too. It's only a matter of time before the heat gets turned back on you and all I'm trying to do is figure out a way to keep it off of you. Now you can pitch a fit, or you can help me help you."

She gaped at his audacity and gave up tying the scarf. "I don't need any help! Especially not from some guy I just met."

He shook his head, his stupid perfect jawline clenching once before saying, "Have you seen the news crews? The wannabe sleuths all over town? Do you want me to read you what they're saying about you?"

Of course she'd seen the crews, but after marrying an abuser, she avoided social media at all costs, and wasn't about to pick up the habit now. *No need to see the perfect life of Claudia from 10th grade on Instagram when I married and then killed a sociopath.* She crossed her arms and refocused.

She needed to get control of this situation fast. "OK, Captain Savior. If you're so sure I killed my husband, how did I do it?"

"That..." He opened his mouth, then shut it. "I don't know."

She pointed her finger and the scarf at him, "Ha! Next question. Why would I kill him?"

His lips formed a straight line and he didn't speak. Her heart sank a little when she realized why. "Because I told you," she said for him. There was no need to hear it from his mouth. "In my garden. I trusted you, and that whole time you were just using it to find a motive?" *You are such an idiot, Maria.* "What about the whole 'sacred space' bit of that conversation? Was that just a bunch of B.S. to get me talking? Were you recording it?"

"Would you just slow down, Maria?" He stepped closer with his hand out like he wanted to touch her but she moved back. He put his hand against his chest instead. "I would never use his abuse against you. And no. I didn't record, nor plan to record, any of our conversations. I actually like our conversations." He ran both hands through his hair, fisting the curled ends. She dragged her eyes away from his biceps filling out his dark gray t-shirt before he dropped his arms. "I'd like to have more conversations with you," he said, resigned.

She ignored that. *He's an actor. He's trying to use you for his show.* "Did you tell anyone about the abuse?"

He paused, and she knew.

"Maria, wait—"

She threw open the door. *You need a plan.*

***

Shane's cameraman, Gary, chain-smoked another round of cigarettes in the van. "Boss isn't going to like this, Shane."

"I'm aware. Frankie seems to dislike everything I do lately," Shane replied, head in his hands. The smoke in the van didn't help his already roiling stomach.

Shane never dealt well with confrontation with anyone, so the fight he and Maria had that morning was putting him over the edge. He popped open the back of the van and grabbed his pullover, desperate for some fresh air. Reporters from all over the state now joined the first wave of wannabe detectives. The picturesque town square was overrun with people Shane had zero interest in interacting with, so he headed in the opposite direction, away from Main Street. His phone started vibrating before he even passed the first block of homes. *Might as well deal with this now.*

"Hi Frankie," he said, already dreading the next four minutes of his life.

"What are you doing?" Frankie shouted through the line. "That last run was even worse than the one before it. You have a homerun in your pocket with that murdered trucker on the heels of Dave Fever and you're phoning it in. I don't even think you did your hair before that last shot. What is *wrong* with you?"

"I told you Frankie, I'm not reading the script they sent over. It isn't Maria Fever. I like the theory of the drug runners, why aren't we running with that?"

"I don't give a damn if Mickey Mouse murdered them. Who cares who actually killed them? I only care about what makes a good story. So if you can make this a good story without the wife, do it. But do it fast, we don't have time on our hands like we normally do."

At some point you were OK with this, Shane thought, disgusted with himself. "Look, we've only taken on cold cases. This isn't my wheelhouse. And regardless of how we've done business in the past, I *need* to find out who is responsible."

"Shane, I invested everything I have in this show. And in you. I don't have the luxury of you suddenly getting a conscious if it means you can't act. You have a contract to fill for this season. Now this running away bit to get your kid's head straight is one thing. I can cover for you for a couple weeks. But more than that? You're going to get yourself in Bravo court and you're dragging me with you."

Shane knew Frankie was right. He should have his attorney look through his contract because the idea of going back to LA right now was off the table. He should also tell Frankie about the kidnapping, but it would only lead to more questions. And once Frankie wanted answers, he didn't stop.

"I have an idea," Shane said, resigned. He hated this idea.

"Does it suck?"

"It'll be good TV."

"Oh yea?" Frankie sounded doubtful, the flick of his lighter clicking in the background. "What is it?"

"I don't think you want to know, but I can't take Gary with me. I need to do this on my own."

Frankie actually paused mid-inhale of another cigarette. "Are you going to take the camera into the morgue?"

"Jeez. No. Why would I do that?" Frankie always pushed the envelope. "No one wants to see dead people."

"It's America, Shane. A lot of us want to see dead people. I already got approval from the only relative Dass has, in case you do." He sounded downright giddy. "You think Maria Fever would give us the green light to show Dave's body?"

"I am not taking a camera into the morgue, Frankie. Just trust me."

"Don't hang—"

Shane hung up. He might be able to kill one bird with two stones, but he'd need black clothes and the GoPro in the van to do it.

***

Maria didn't think her day could get much worse, but Rosa Cruz had a way of surprising her.

She was helpful that way.

"Mama, why are there rosaries on my walls?" She asked as she dropped her keys into their spot by the door.

Rosa either ignored her or didn't hear so Maria looked to Isa. Isa shook her head back and forth as if in warning.

Maria touched her mother's shoulder, only to realize she wasn't just muttering to herself... she was praying in Spanish. That was never a good sign.

"What happened?" Maria asked.

Isa swung her legs back and forth under the round breakfast table, causing her pile of color pencils to quiver. She looked up for a minute and said, "Abuelita said something about El Diablo coming to town? I dunno."

Isa shrugged and went back to coloring, but at the

mention of the Devil, Rosa crossed herself and prayed faster. "Okay..." Maria said. "Isa, why don't you give me and Abuelita a minute? I saw that Evelyn and Cindy are home from their cruise."

Isa squealed and ran out the door to find her favorite neighbors. Maria shouted after her, "Hug them hello for me!"

She turned, hands on hips, and said, "Enough, Mama. God doesn't care if we have more rosaries."

"You clearly haven't watched the news then, *mija*," Rosa said, finally pausing her prayer.

"I'm actively avoiding the news lately, but I promise to watch it again if they catch the devil walking down Main Street."

"This is not a joke," Rosa hissed. "They're saying it's a cult." She clicked her heels over to her fuchsia purse and grabbed her phone. Rosa waved the pink case in front of Maria's face. "Read this and then you'll be grateful for my rosaries."

"Facts 4Ever Media? Really, Mama? I thought we were past this. Just because someone has a website does not mean they're telling the truth. Look here. Their first headline is that the president is doing experiments on kittens in the basement of the White House. I'm pretty sure we can ignore anything else."

"Scroll down," Rosa said, her toes tapping on the old hardwood floors.

Maria huffed out a breath and read aloud:

"Quaint New England Town Home to Murdering Satanic Cult"

Rosa waved her on to continue, so Maria rolled her eyes and kept going.

"At approximately 6:45 a.m. EST the corpse of murdered Dave Fever was discovered in a SATANIC RITUAL at Memorial Hospital in Western Vermont. This comes days after the grisly murder of Massachusetts man, Nathan Dass. Locals on the ground believe a SATANIC CULT is afoot in the charming New England town of Hinnewatcha—"

Maria paused. "Why do they keep capitalizing the satanic bits?

Rosa swatted her and took the phone, "Now are you happy with the rosaries?"

"It's not a cult," Maria replied. "The police think it's just a bunch of kids messing around with Halloween pranks."

"What about 'Satan's Hand?'"

Maria rubbed at her temples. "I have no idea what you're talking about, Mama, and this has been an awful morning."

"Nathan Dass," Rosa said, arms out as if Maria was the biggest moron in town. "His name is an anagram. It spells out Satan's Hand if you rearrange it."

Maria snorted, only to get swatted again by her mother.

"It's not funny, Maria! Someone did a satanic ritual on your husband's dead body, and then they murdered their own member at the only gas station *you* go to."

"Dan's Diesel is literally the only gas station in town, Mama. It's the only gas station all Hinnewatchans go to." Maria needed something stronger than tea and made her way to the kitchen.

Rosa's heels clicked right behind her, shooting tiny shock waves to the headache building in Maria's head. "Then why is there a cop parked outside our house?"

Maria dodged that one as she rifled through her shelves for a wine glass. "Eh, they're just being cautious since the murder. More cops on all streets type thing." The last thing Rosa Cruz needed to hear right now is that Maria thought she was being followed.

She looked like she didn't believe her in the slightest, but she let it go. Instead, her mother took her by the shoulders, forcing her to pause her rifling in the cabinets. "Maria, I failed you once. I turned my back on you when you needed me the most."

"What are you talking about, Mama?" Maria softened. She rarely saw her mother tear up. She raged, she laughed, she loved hard, and hovered like hell, but Rosa Cruz was not a crier. She took her mother's manicured hand in her own. "You never failed me."

Rosa looked up to the kitchen ceiling as if gravity would push her tears back in. She used the edge of her hot pink pinky nail to fix her winged eyeliner and said, "I did. Two years ago when you and Isa needed a place to stay I told you no. I'd read all these parenting books and I thought it was tough love. I should have–"

"Mama, no. I needed to find my own place to land, and it wasn't going to be my mother's house. And because of that, I found this town and–"

"And Dave," Rosa interrupted, shaking her head and thumping her tanned fist against her own chest, her gold bracelets banging together. "You found Dave because *I* was too angry to let you come home. If I just let you come home, you wouldn't have had to–"

Maria held her hand up before she could say the words that Maria dreaded the most. If her mother knew, if she aided her cover up in any way, Isa might not be able to go to her if the worst happened and Maria was arrested. She drew back her shoulders and looked at her mother unflinchingly. "Mama, I need you to listen to me. The rash girl that left home before finishing high school to follow some boy is gone. The girl that would take the first man that offered even a smidge of kindness is gone. And the woman that put up with any man that hurt her or threatened her child is now dead."

Rosa's face crumpled. Maria didn't tell her about Dave's abuse, but she found out towards the end regardless. It was her stupid pride, and misplaced shame, that made her feel like she couldn't ask for help when she needed it the most. But she imagined that her mother knew something was amiss when she made excuses to not go home or allow her to come visit. She had already begun plans to get Dave in the ground by the day Rosa walked in and saw the bruises while she changed shirts. Any arguments and anger they'd harbored about their past were forgotten then, and her mother's words that day had become a mantra to her in the following weeks. *Never again.*

Maria squeezed her mother's shoulders so she would look at her. "Do you remember what I told you that day when you wanted to go to the cops?"

"To trust you," Rosa said quietly. "That you were fixing the problem."

"Exactly," Maria said, nodding. "And now I need you

to trust me again when I tell you that I am fixing the problem. I know you think this house is a wreck. I know you think my life is a disaster, and believe me," she laughed and pushed back at her own watering eyes. "I know, more than anyone, that elements of my life have been disastrous. But no more. I am capable of protecting myself and Isa, and no one, not even a Satanic cult, will change that now."

"I never doubted you, Maria," her mother said as she cradled her hands on either side of Maria's face. "You are a great mother, and a woman that every great, single man within a hundred miles of here should be tripping over themselves just to talk to." She smiled, and cocked one arched eyebrow up as she continued, "Obviously. You are my daughter after all."

They laughed and each dried their eyes. Her mother cleared her throat after a few moments and said, "But I still want us to wear these." She held up two red string bracelets and wiggled them in front of Maria. "Isa already has hers on."

"Mama," Maria chided as she finally retrieved the wine glass from the back of the cabinet. She poured a glass of rosé from the bottle she opened the night before. "*You* were the one that said Lita was a superstitious old coot and laughed when I came home with my Mal de Ojo bracelet."

Rosa sniffed, "Yeah, well I learned too late that my mother was always right. You should learn from my mistakes."

"Fine," Maria said as she slipped her bracelet on. She saluted her mother with the glass and the wrist that now held the Mal de Ojo bracelet and headed for the back door.

Her mother called out, " Now where are you going?"

"To the garden, Mama. I love you, but I need to think."

"The Mayor is calling another Town Meeting tonight," Rosa said before the door shut. "We should go."

"Then I am definitely going to need more wine," Maria said, backtracking for the full bottle. She tucked the cold rosé bottle under her arm and grabbed the slim notepad covered in flowers she kept by the door along with her favorite pen. She had another list to make for tonight's preparations.

11

Methy in the Best Way

SHANE PARKED HIS CAR on the side of the road a bit past the turn off for Greg Fever's farm. He clutched the GoPro camera in his hand, wincing at the gravel crunching with every step he took in between the tall, quiet woods.

Vermont was the second least populated state in the US, topping only Wyoming. He didn't have to go far out of town to feel like he was in the boonies, and Greg lived a solid hike outside of town. And up a long hill. He paused to catch his breath and checked his watch for the hundredth time. *In and out, under an hour, regardless of what I do, or don't, find. The Town Hall meeting should last at least an hour.*

He didn't tell his dad his plans. The stubborn old man would just try to come if he couldn't stop Shane. So, he texted Gary once more to reconfirm that he spotted Greg in the crowd. *Text me if he leaves the room.*

Greg Fever had removed any trace of plants or grass at the top of the hill where his RV was parked. A yellowing trailer with a gash down one side sat opposite the RV, and a collection of tires and broken down cars formed a semi circle around them. A trash can fire still smoldered off to the side, and a few glass bottles were scattered around an old folding chair aimed at a wide fire pit.

Darkness settled an hour before, but Shane could see well enough with the moonlight and contractor lights that Greg had staged around his fiefdom.

Alllllright. No going back now.

He strapped the GoPro on his head, cringing despite being alone. The Hi-ho song from Snow White would be stuck in his head for hours after he wore the camera on his forehead. Shane turned the camera on, its beam illuminating a few paces ahead of him, and made a wide circle around the RV and the trailer to make sure there were no surprises lurking. He planned to voice over the film later, so the only noise audible besides the occasional owl was his panting breath.

Shane entered the RV first. Shoes, piles of dirty dishes, and fast food trash greeted him. He tried to block out the smell of sweat and feet as he walked from one end of the RV to the other. *What were you expecting? A treasure box of pills labeled "illegal"?*

He opened the few drawers and kitchen cabinets, half expecting a rat to jump out at any moment, but turned up empty. With a groan he put his hands on the floor, avoiding a sticky patch by sheer dumb luck, and checked under the couch/dining room bench. Nothing. He panned the GoPro light under Greg's bed and it bounced off a long black case.

Please don't get stuck, please don't get stuck. He used a hanger and his freakishly long arms to drag the case towards him without getting fully wedged underneath. He turned the three digit dials to 1-2-3. No luck. He tried a few more combinations and almost shoved it back before trying 0-0-0. It clicked just as he thought he heard something outside the trailer.

Freezing, he crouched down in between the bed and the wall and turned off the GoPro so his light wouldn't give him away. He flicked the metal blinds open a fraction to see out the front. *No one is here. You'd hear a car drive up if it was Greg.* After a few more minutes of stillness and no sounds he turned on the camera again and cracked open the case. A mess of batteries, portable speakers, and several small black boxes with red and black wires were inside. He pushed a stray wire back, shutting the case, and the sound of loud heavy breathing bounced off the too-close walls.

He startled, banging his head against the window. Sheer panic had to die down before he realized it was just one of the black boxes making the breathing sounds. *What the hell?* He took one out and slipped it into his pocket, shoving the case back where he found it. He waited outside the RV in the still air for his heart to finally stop racing.

I'm too old for this, he thought, as he turned the knob to the busted trailer. No lights came on, so he turned on the light on his GoPro. Despite the gash down the side of it, the trailer was significantly cleaner than the RV. There was no trash on the floor, and the low twin bed was made. A neat pile of folded men's shirts sat on the counter, and the same moment Shane recognized the gray and black flannel shirt on top, he heard a creak behind him.

He turned just in time to block the baseball bat swung at him, but the momentum knocked his camera off his head. The front door to the trailer was open now, spilling moonlight over his attacker. He could make out a smaller figure, dressed in head to toe black, with a ski mask on. Dark curls poked out of the bottom of the mask.

"Maria?" He asked, incredulous.

She stopped yanking on the bat he still held and ripped off the ski mask.

"Jesus on a stick! You scared the hell out of me," she said, but she hugged him, briefly and tight before pulling back.

"What are you doing here?" She loud-whispered.

He picked up his GoPro and lamely held it aloft. "I thought I'd find the drugs Madison thinks Greg and Dave stole. I hoped to get something on camera so we could get Dave's case off you."

Maria shook her head, exasperation in every quaking curl. "We have to get out of here. Do you recognize those clothes?" She pointed at the pile behind Shane with her bat.

"I think so. Tat Face?" At her nod, he continued, "Text Madison to see where he is. They're supposed to be tailing that guy." He pulled out his phone. "I've got someone watching—"

His stomach dropped. He'd missed a text from Gary 10 minutes ago. "How long does it take to get to Town Hall from here?"

"Maybe fifteen minutes," Maria said. "Why?"

"We have to get out of here."

"That's what I said!" Maria whisper-shouted.

As if he conjured Greg with his thoughts, headlights filtered through the trees. The distinct sound of tires on gravel echoed in the too-quiet woods.

They bolted.

Maria grabbed his hand and yanked Shane in the woods behind the trailer, past the smoldering trash fire. They ran until they heard the car turn off, and the pair ducked behind trees. They were far too close to the trailer for Shane's comfort.

"Yea?" Shane heard the man say before pausing. "No, not today. Yea. I'll call you when I do."

He risked a peek from behind the tree, and watched the man with the tattoos on his face walk to the trailer. He mouthed to Maria, "It's Tat Face," and her mouthed response looked eerily like, "No shit."

He realized then that neither of them thought to shut the trailer door. Tat Face must have realized something was off in the same moment because he suddenly stopped walking. Shane risked another quick glimpse behind the trees only to see Tat Face creeping around the side of the trailer. The moonlight caught on the metal in his hands and Shane almost pissed himself at the size of the knife.

Maria was as still as the tree behind her, eyes pinched closed. He knew Brandon would take care of Emily but he would have given anything to be able to give her a hug one more time. He didn't risk another look, he could hear Tat Face slowly circling the trailer by the crunch in the leaves.

Shane would fight. He didn't stand much of a chance, but he had the element of surprise and it would at least be enough for Maria to run like hell. He started breathing heavier, in and out. *I can do this.*

He glanced at Maria who was looking at him like he was crazy and shaking her head vehemently no. She held a hand up, *Wait.*

He couldn't hear leaves crunching anymore. *Tat Face is probably waiting behind his trailer, watching us.*

New headlights beamed against the trees again down the hill, and he heard Tat Face start walking around again to the front of his trailer. It sounded like a truck, playing Noah Kahan, was pulling up the gravel drive. Maria and Shane didn't wait. She grabbed his hand and led him down a path he never would have noticed in the dark. The two crouched as low as they could and scrambled down the side of the hill through the trees.

Neither spoke, and Shane was convinced that at any moment they'd hear Tat Face shout out. After what felt like an eternity, the path opened up to a small parking lot. Maria's rusty Honda gleamed under the moonlight like the rescue horse it was, and they ran to it. She threw it in reverse, and the car bumped over dips and divots before turning onto the smooth, curvy road.

She spoke then, still a little breathless. "Greg's place backs up to that state park. Dave and I used to hike that path when we first met."

"Handy." He looked at her, and held his hand out, palm up. "Let's never do that again, ok?"

She put her hand in his and squeezed it once. "Deal." She dropped his hand, turning up the heat instead, and said, "I think we should get some coffee."

"And vodka," Shane added. "Or Baileys, or bourbon. I'd do wine, too. Tequila?"

"I know a place that has all of that," Maria said, as she hugged the curvy roads that led back to town.

12

CONFESSIONAL WINE

MARIA NESTLED INTO HER favorite spot at Mama Cate's. The bistro table had barely enough room for two, but it was close to the small fireplace and partially hidden from the rest of the store by the Historical Romance bookshelf.

"Thanks Nina," she said, taking the two glasses of wine the college kid delivered. The girl that manned the shop most evenings did a double take at Shane as he walked back from the bathroom. Maria didn't blame her. Shane was comically attractive. The kind of attractive only seen on TV—good cheekbones, broad shoulders, and the easy smile you could show off to your parents or lose your mind over in bed.

He didn't notice Maria ogling him while he attempted to fold himself into the corner. He seemed to settle on stretching his long legs out along one side of her, angled towards the smuttiest books in the shop.

"Sorry," she said. "This is my favorite spot. I didn't think about someone over 5ft 2 sitting here."

"I love it," he said, waving her off and resting his hands

on his stomach. He looked perfectly at ease lounging in her spot.

She took a sip of her wine as he squinted at the shelves behind her. He asked, "Is that book really called, *The Dirtiest Billionaire?*"

Maria snorted. "Yes, it's part of the Bad Boys of Boulevard series. I'm pretty sure there are at least a few copies left if you want one."

"Nope, I'm good," he said, chuckling.

She wasn't ready to dive into what they were both doing at Greg's place, or acknowledge his claim that he was there to get Dave's case off her. Maria realized it was hard to stay mad at him, despite her best efforts.

So she told him about the Book Club instead. "Our most popular book club comes in after bridge on the last Thursday of the month. It's a pack of old biddies that try to one up each other with the filthiest lines from those books."

She set her wine glass aside so her hands wouldn't knock it over. It was impossible to talk about this group without some animation. "They start drinking at bridge so most are tipsy when they walk in. Mind you, this is *maybe* three o'clock in the afternoon. They claim they're just retelling the most romantic lines, but everyone knows the smuttiest ones win. Whomever they deem the winner has to stand up and wave something like their scarf or jacket over their heads while everyone else chants her name. On one particularly late Book Club, one of the oldest women there took off her bra through a sleeve and waved it around like a helicopter."

"Shut up," Shane said, laughing. "I don't think I want to know who. What do the men say when they're in here?"

"Are you kidding me, on that Thursday? Every Hinnewatchan male knows to stay away. The only one brave enough is Hamby, and that's just because if it gets too unruly he knows that Cate will ditch the barista counter to join them and he'll need to man the place solo."

He laughed out loud, so clear and full of joy that she leaned in conspiratorially. "Do you want to know a secret?"

Shane quieted and leaned closer, "Always."

"I caught Hamby reading one of their books behind his paper."

He leaned back, belly laughing. A few tables were taken by college kids and teenagers, or regulars lost in their own books. The fire to her side crackled and she realized that Mama Cate's had become a sort of shelter for her in the last few months. She loved coming here alone to this table to curl up with a book on her break, but seeing Shane across from her felt right despite all the reasons why it shouldn't. She tried to ignore it, but the more time she spent with him, the harder it became to keep her secrets from him.

His laughter died down, and they sat in companionable silence for a beat as he toyed with the frayed edge of a napkin. "I always thought I'd turn into a Hamby," he said quietly.

She cocked her head, not following, so he explained in between sips of wine. "Like old-man-love content. The kind of guy that loves even just being in the room with his old and gray wife. Hamby's been like that for decades. Have you seen the way he still looks at Cate?"

"Oh I know, it's enough to make you swoon," Maria said. "I always thought they fit like puzzle pieces. She's all sharp edges and loud and crass, and he's quiet and patient and lets her shove her way into any conversation." She watched the firewood burn for a minute and embraced the wine warming her veins. "Do you think you'll still find your Cate?"

He didn't answer right away, but watched her with the same intensity that he had in her garden when she all but spilled her darkest secrets to him. She hadn't known him long, but she felt completely at ease with him. The feeling was unnerving.

Shane cleared his throat and answered, "I think I will. But I don't think she'll be in LA."

Mama Cate's after dinner crowd had trickled out while they talked, so only a couple patrons remained, their conversations murmured. Nina played Paolo Nutini's *Autumn Leaves* on low, and Shane added another gnarled log to the fire next to them.

Maria waited for the crackling flames to settle back down before she spoke again. "If she's not in LA, will you go back there when this is all done?"

He ripped at the corner of the paper napkin now, slow and deliberate so that one side fringed. "I used to think that living anywhere but LA, New York, or Chicago was too boring. But the older I get, and more importantly, the older Emily gets, the more I realize I've overlooked the charms of a small town."

She had hoped for a minute that he would say that town was Hinnewatcha specifically. Even foolishly wished that he'd hint that she was reason enough to stay in this particular small town. *You married someone so atrocious that murder was the only way out, Maria. Pretty sure the models and actresses he's used to don't have that type of baggage. Besides, the last thing you need is another man in your life.*

Nina walked over then, disrupting Maria's headfirst dive into self-pity. "Hey Maria, you think you can lock up when you leave? I have a date and that last couple over there just paid the tab."

"No problem, Nina. Have fun and I'll take care of everything."

Nina walked out to kiss a young man waiting for her on the sidewalk. Maria shook off the tinge of jealousy and focused instead on the good man in front of her. He wasn't hers, he had no obligations to her, and yet he still went to dangerous lengths to help her. She stood up and fetched the rest of the bottle from the counter, lost in thought.

She'd binge watched his show in her room every night the last week, and no episode had him looting through potential drug dealers' homes on behalf of a bereaved family. She could distrust him like she'd distrusted most men before her, but she was tired. Tired of being paranoid. Tired of men disappointing her, hurting her. But she'd never thought all men were bad. Even in the depths of misery with Dave, she knew good men were out there. She'd just let herself believe for some insane reason that she only deserved Dave.

She'd come to the conclusion in the garden earlier that, despite how wrong it looked on paper, she trusted Shane to help. She knew she could figure this out without his assistance, but she didn't have to. Asking for help wasn't a sign of weakness, and some fights don't have to be fought alone. And she'd fought on her own unnecessarily for too long.

The wine also helped loosen her tongue.

"I don't know why, Shane, but I trust you," she said as she sat back down and topped off their glasses.

He quickly looked away from the fire and focused that intensity on her, so she went on before she could lose her nerve. She took a deep breath. "I killed my husband."

Tears threatened to spring, so she willed them into the back of her head as she chuckled, "Wow. That felt surprisingly good to say out loud."

Shane leaned forward, taking her hands in his across the table. "Thank you for telling me that. And I should have talked to you first, but you can trust me and my family. We'll protect you, Maria. No one will find out if I can do anything about it."

"Why?" Maria asked, knowing she should take her hands back but not quite ready to do so. She also knew she shouldn't kick a gift horse in the mouth, but she was weary of those horses because some nasty ones had left their mark. "Why are you protecting me? You could be done with your show, done with this town, and not implicate yourself in the process by turning me in."

"Because, despite us not knowing each other well, I trust you, too. And I don't care how you did it, but if you felt cornered enough that the only way out was killing him, I'm ok with that."

She wanted to curl up in his arms and have a solid cry, but she ignored that urge. She shifted her hands out of his, and asked, "So, now what?"

"Now, you and I will figure out a plan. Walk me through your conversation with Chief Madison one more time?"

***

Shane hadn't registered how bad he wanted Maria to trust him until she confessed. He hadn't known her long, but he wanted her to know that he'd do everything he could to protect her. In the span of just a few days she'd become someone he wanted to be around, despite his best attempts to ignore it. He wanted to talk to her, to hear her unfettered laugh. He cared about women before her, but not with the same intensity or escalation. All the nausea he'd felt raging since their fight dissipated, and the problems they needed to address suddenly seemed surmountable instead of impossible.

He listened to her recap, trying not to get distracted by the way she bit her full bottom lip when she was in thought, or the way her soft curves looked in the firelight. He'd dated his fair share of decent and horrible women back in LA, but the last thing Maria needed was his baggage dropped at her front door. She had enough on her plate, and had for some time now. He couldn't imagine putting her in danger simply because he kept wondering what it'd be like to have her in his arms. But he, selfishly, could use a friend.

He'd lost touch with the friends he'd made in this town decades ago, and most had moved away not long after him. Shane was chummy with a handful of his coworkers, but there was no one he'd call if he ran out of sugar. Let alone call to work through his myriad of kidnapper, murders, and poltergeist problems. He felt like Maria would help him work through any problem.

"What?" Maria asked, stopping her recap midway. "Why are you smiling?"

"Sorry. It's just that I'm glad you're not mad at me anymore. I like having you as a friend."

He didn't recognize the look that brushed over her face, so he pushed on with what they needed to discuss. "OK. Back to business. Tat Face is living on Greg's property. Even if what the mayor says is true and all the short term properties are taken, why would he do that? The next town's only an hour from here. There must be at least some rooms to rent there."

"I don't know," Maria said. "Maybe like calls to like? One shady fellow feels more comfortable with another?"

"Or, he's not in town for you," Shane said, "but because he's involved with Greg's side drug business. Chief Madison said Greg served time for minor dealing years ago. Maybe they met there."

"Or he could be staying near Greg to see if he has the stash of pills Levi thinks they stole. Maybe he's from another gang and is waiting to make his move to hurt Greg."

"We'll need to talk to Madison soon about this," Shane said, his mind stuck on her word choice. *Gang.* He lingered on another reason Tat Face could be in town, gut sinking, but pushed past that for the moment.

Maria nodded, quiet for a minute. "Shane, if Greg and Dave stole drugs from the wrong guy, would that be enough for the police to assume Dave was murdered because of it?"

"I think so," Shane replied as he leaned back in the small space. "It doesn't have to be true. Just murky enough to take the most likely suspect, which is always the spouse, off the table."

He crossed his arms, not wanting to push her away but

he had to ask. "Maria, I went through Dave's files. Why didn't you go to the police when Dave first hit you?"

She grew quiet before answering. "The first couple times I really thought it was a fluke. He was so sorry, so apologetic, crying—the works. We'd go months where nothing happened, and then he'd come home loaded and fly off the handle. He was always brimming with anger, but it was subtle at first. I thought it was something I did wrong. Some—" she waved her hand in the air and shook her head. "— deficiency on my end that if I just fixed it, if I just stopped, I could keep that anger from spilling over."

She held her hand up, incorrectly assuming he'd interrupt her. She continued, "I know now how ridiculous that sounds. It took some soul searching, some time, and a hell of a lot of self-help podcasts, but I started to build my confidence and expectations back up, in spite of being married to him. I brought up divorce, and he said he'd never leave his town, his house. That I was his. That I should be grateful for the mortgage and bills that I split, because I'd been desperate when we first arrived. Apparently, "divorce" wasn't in his family's vocabulary, as if they were some Camelot of aspiration. I realized then that I'd never be truly free of him, so I went to the cops—it was before Levi was there. The chief at the time came to my house. I didn't realize he was Dave's friend's dad. He didn't write a report, just promised to have a chat with Dave."

What a bastard, Shane thought, grateful again for Levi Madison taking over. "Let me guess, the chat didn't help?"

"That's an understatement. Dave laughed that time, said no one would believe me because he never hit my face.

I think that was the night I decided enough was enough. We had to leave." Maria stood up and locked the door as the last couple left, turned off the open sign, and sat back down across from him. He sat on his hands so he wouldn't try to pull her to him as she breathed out a weary sigh before continuing. She watched the table as she continued. "I packed our bags while Isa was at a friend's house and Dave was supposed to be at work. My plan was to pick Isa up and head straight to my aunt's. He knew my mom's address, but not hers."

"The bags were on the kitchen table when he came home early. I didn't hear him pull up. I had gone to Evelyn & Cindy's to leave a note at their back door. But that also meant that I didn't hear Isa come home early, too." Shane covered his mouth, but didn't stop her. He recognized that she needed to say her story so he stayed silent even as her words wrecked him.

"I walked in to find all hell had broken loose. He's screaming in Isa's face, as if any of this was her doing, and I pushed him. I shoved him as hard as I could and he was angrier than I'd ever seen. I told Isa to go next door, but she put herself between us. He'd turned on the stove at some point, and so when he shoved her out of the way she hit her hand on the hot stove. She still has the burn marks on her knuckles."

Maria crossed her arms tight against her chest, and Shane couldn't stop himself from dragging his chair to be next to her. He didn't move to touch her, and stayed quiet while she decided if she wanted to keep going or not. She cleared her throat and continued, still not meeting his eyes.

"He stormed out after, shouting something about Isa knowing her place and that he'd make sure she learned it. He took my keys and my cell phone that night. Said he'd always find me, no matter where I went. It didn't matter. The moment I saw him in Isa's face I knew what I needed to do."

"I mapped out a plan in the back of my mind for months, just in case. I think mentally listing out all the steps that might need to happen put me at ease, so it was just a matter of ticking through that list."

"By that time," she continued, her gaze steady on the fire, "the old police chief retired to Florida, which helped. Getting around someone that was vested in Dave was always going to be problematic. I knew Greg could be an issue, but not as much as a cop. They brought Levi in from somewhere else, and I could tell he was different, would be on my side. But I didn't want to wait around for the court system to fix a problem I knew how to resolve. Dave was never the type to honor a restraining order anyway. I was determined to see Dave put in the ground." She looked at him then, her gaze unflinching. "So I did."

"I'm glad you did," Shane said, trying to tamp down the anger he wanted to unleash on a dead man. "You don't have to tell me how if you're not comfortable, but it might help if I know the whole picture."

She nodded, "It's fine. I don't plan on ever repeating this story to anyone and it feels cathartic to run through it once aloud." She blew out a breath, her face framing curls dancing for a moment.

"I learned that Dave was deathly allergic to almonds a

few months prior. So I made sure I worked an evening shift on the night when Isa had a slumber party at a friend's house. But before I left, I injected every pill he kept in his coat pocket, every pill he ferreted away in the house, and every bottle of liquor we had with a tiny bit of almond oil. Enough to cause a reaction that would have him reaching for his Epipen that I filled to the brim with almond oil. I made plans to have wine at Evelyn and Cindy's and play cards with their friends after my shift ended, but before I walked into their home and with all those people that would vouch for my whereabouts, I slipped in my back door."

"Dave always took a couple pills after his shift, you could set your watch to it, and he always washed them down with whatever booze we had. It was no surprise that his body was already cold by the time I snuck in. I put on latex gloves I'd brought home from Cate's and injected him with a syringe of Valium that he thought he hid from me. And then I texted Greg from Dave's phone to come over. I took the Epipen and the gloves and threw them away in Evelyn's outside trash can, and walked through their front door right on time."

Shane was morbidly impressed, and said as much. "It should have worked."

"It should have worked," Maria echoed, nodding. "But I wasn't expecting Greg to get so involved. Honestly, it's like he's more clear now than he ever was when Dave was alive. And I assumed, after what felt like months of researching, that a full syringe of Valium would be enough to make any coroner call it an overdose."

Shane ripped up another napkin as he worked through everything she'd told him and how they could get caught. He asked after a moment,"Do you know what he and Greg did whenever they were up at the farm?"

She shook her head. "No. I avoided him as much as I could so whenever he left the house I didn't question it. But he seemed to have more cash on him," She stopped Shane before he got too excited, "Not like tons. He was always paycheck to paycheck. But enough that he was planning to fix up his truck with these ridiculous tires and lights."

"That might be enough. Hell," Shane said, running a hand through his hair and leaning back. "He might have actually stolen the drugs. He was obviously stupid enough not to realize that by some miracle he'd landed a perfect woman. I wouldn't put it past him to steal from a bigger dealer."

Maria blushed and he leaned in again. She knew it, but he wanted to remind her that Dave was an insecure, terrible man. And that not all men were like that. But his cell phone buzzed with a text and he glanced down. He could feel the blood draining from his face.

"What is it?" Maria asked, concerned.

"It's Emily. She's in trouble, and I don't have my car."

Maria threw a cup of water on the fire, its steam hissing away the cozy warmth in an instant. "I'll drive, we'll get your car in the morning."

Shane tried to ignore the carousel of terrible what-ifs as they locked up behind them as fast as they could. He barely heard Maria's conversation with the 9-1-1 operator as she pulled out of the parking spot. Every time he reread Emily's text his fear grew.

Help. Hiding at D's Diesel. Something in the woods.

13

Ghosts at the Gas Station

FOG ROLLED OFF THE mountains, hovering over the curvy road and blurring the forest around them. The typically cheery lights on the red barn of Dan's Diesel were just hazy blobs of half light by the time Maria pulled her car in the gas station.

One light was on inside, and the only other car apart from hers was a beat up pick up truck parked at the edge of the property near the entrance to the Burial Rock Trail. Shane jumped out of the passenger seat as soon as her car stopped. She followed him to the door, pulling her heavy cardigan tighter in the wind, and winced at the banging in the too-quiet night.

"Emily! Open up! It's me." He said, yanking on the front door as if he could pry the locked door open with just an arm.

Maria offered, "Call her again? I'll check the other entrance around the side."

She walked around the building, shivering at the now

empty space where the trucker was murdered. The side door was locked, but before she turned away she thought she heard whispers.

"Hello? Emily?"

Stupid kids. Why would they come out here when we just had a murder?

She kept her voice steady, belying her nerves. "Emily, it's Maria Fever. Your dad is here too, you can come out now."

She crept around to the back, attempting to keep her footsteps light. The gas station backed up to a retaining wall and the dark woods behind it loomed over the little red hut. She could just make out a few empty blue pallets leaning against a storage shed under the back door's flickering light. Maria scanned the woods for any movement or any more whispers, but heard nothing. She twisted the Mal de Ojo bracelet around her wrist, trying and failing to ignore her mother's fears. *Satanic cult. Satanic rituals.*

An empty glass bottle rolled over the pavement in the wind, and she knocked over a crate in her haste to get out of the narrow space with too little light. She threw out her arms to regain her balance just as someone grabbed her from behind.

Maria opened her mouth to scream in the same moment she registered Shane's voice behind her. "Shh, it's just me."

Heart racing, she turned around in his arms and hugged him tight. "Sorry, Shane. I got freaked out." His arms tightened around her, and she buried her face in his pullover. She breathed in its crisp linen scent before reluctantly pulling back. "Come on, that door is locked. Let's go back to my car while we wait for the cops."

He shook his head, whispering back. "You go wait in the car for them. I'm going to check the trail to Burial Rock. I don't know what Emily is doing, but she overheard some teenagers talking about it. She wouldn't let it go earlier. I think she might have gone there."

"On her own? I doubt—" Maria was interrupted at the thump from the storage shed. Shane pushed her behind him as the shed door creaked open.

In the dim light Maria could just make out Emily's light blonde hair and at least a couple more teenagers. "Dad?" Emily asked.

"Oh thank God, " Shane said in a sigh, closing the distance to them in just a few strides. He scooped Emily up, her short legs dangling a foot above the pavement. *She must have been terrified if she allowed him to squeeze her like that in front of the others.*

"Danny?" Maria asked, as the gas station attendant walked out of the shed. He looked paler than normal, and two more teens she didn't recognize followed behind him.

Danny crossed his arms tightly in his oversized coat, chewing on his lip piercing. "Honey, are you ok?" Maria asked, looking everyone over.

"Mrs. Fever, we were out at Burial Rock." He glanced back at the dark woods as one of the girls behind him began to cry. He stepped closer to Maria and whispered, "Something isn't right."

Maria ignored the warning bells clanging in her head and his stiffness as she pulled him into a quick hug. She put her arms around the other girls as well and said, "OK, everybody inside. The cops are already on their way and we'll call your parents. You can explain what's wrong inside where it's warm." *And less creepy.*

Danny pulled keys from his pocket to unlock the back door, the key slipping on the lock before it opened. Maria wondered if his hand was shaking from the cold or nerves, and forced herself to not glance back at the woods behind them again. She flipped on every switch inside, illuminating the old black and white checkered laminate floors and rows of sundries and snacks. Rusted metal signs hung from any available inch of wall space, and the mahogany counter gleamed under the lights. Shane's usually cheerful eyes were on his daughter as they walked in. Maria pushed the heavy metal door closed behind him, the snip of the deadbolt echoing in the silent shop.

Danny turned on the ancient coffee pot behind the counter, and with the familiar gurgle of heating water in the background, Emily began to pace in front of Shane. "Dad, I'm sorry, I know I shouldn't have snuck out. I met Danny and his friends earlier this week, and we all got to talking about Burial Rock and the Abenaki tribe. They know so much about the history, and when I said I was interested, they let me tag along for a bonfire at the end of the trail. It was just supposed to be something low key, we all planned to be home before midnight."

The teen girls behind Emily nodded along emphatically, their heavy eyeliner streaked from crying. Maria was grateful she had a little while longer with Isa while she still slept in emoji footed pajamas and loved unicorn coloring books.

Shane huffed out a sigh in a way that only a frustrated parent could. "Emily. I care less about the time and more about the fact that someone was murdered right here less than a week ago. We still don't know who did it. What part of that seemed ok to ignore and go on a hike in the woods surrounding *the murder site* at night?"

"I know! I'm sorry. It was just something stupid. Everyone said you could only see The Protector in the fall. So when I found the ouija board in town I thought—"

Maria snorted. "Really kids? You guys honestly believe in ghosts?" She tried to forget the fact that she'd had nightmares of Dave coming back to life the night before.

The Bolles pair shared a look, and Maria cocked her head at Shane. "Please tell me you don't too."

Shane said, "Of course not," but he didn't meet her eyes. He glared at Emily, "Seriously? A ouija board. Did you give a Magic 8 Ball a good shake beforehand too?"

Any remorse from Emily evaporated at Shane's sarcasm. She crossed her arms and leveled him a look that spelled trouble. "*Some* people think the spirit of an Abenaki woman can be found at the end of the trail. And *some* people think that spirit is trying to warn this town about the murders. And some–"

"I've heard enough," Shane said, his usual affable smile gone. "Drop it, Emily."

"Not until you hear this," Emily jerked her head towards Danny behind the counter. "Go on, tell the great Detective Shane Bolles here what you told me earlier."

Danny seemed to shrink down into his hoodie. Emily rolled her eyes. "Ugh fine. I'll do it. Danny was telling us about things his family has seen in the woods lately. Like even before the murder. Lights in the woods, voices at night. We wanted to check it out for ourselves."

Danny muttered, "My parents are going to kill me."

"Just want to make sure I have all this straight," Shane said, fisting his hands at his sides. "You snuck out of the house so you could check out the voices someone heard in the woods…away from any help…near an active murder scene, and the only thing you brought with you was a oujia board?"

The taller of the blonde girls raised her hand, "I brought snacks?"

"Lovely, " Shane deadpanned. "Thank you. At least you weren't going to starve before the murderer found you in the woods."

Maria took a step towards Shane and put her hand on his back before she could stop herself. He seemed to lean into her touch as she asked, "Emily, is that what your text was about? Did you hear voices while you were out there?"

Emily gave Maria a small nod, likely grateful her dad would have to wait before he could rile himself up even more. "Well, we didn't hear voices per se... But when we got the fire lit, we heard something else."

Danny blurted, "It was breathing. Like heavy breathing, not from a dog or from any other animal."

Shane stilled, and Maria asked, "Could it have been a bear?"

The kids shrugged, but Emily said, "That's just it. We didn't hear any other movement. Like no leaves shuffling, no footsteps. Silence. But the breathing still moved all around us. And then we saw–"

Headlights swept over the storefront, interrupting her. Danny's heavy-set dad barreled out of his truck a moment later, gun in hand. Shane pushed Emily behind him, but Maria shrugged him off when he reached for her as well. "It's just Danny's dad, Chris," she said to Shane as she walked to the front door. She held it open for Chris and he rushed in, nodding once to her.

"Danny?" Chris asked, setting the rifle on the countertop before walking behind it.

The pair hugged, and whatever Danny said was muffled in between his dad's arms. Chris walked back around and shook Shane's hand, introducing himself as his son passed the girls Styrofoam cups of coffee.

"Thanks for getting here so fast," Chris said. "I didn't see Danny's text until ten minutes ago. This is my dad's place, by the way."

Shane nodded, his arm still around Emily's shoulders. "Nice to meet you, wish it was under different circumstances but the kids seem ok. Just a little spooked."

A deputy pulled up a moment later and the girls and Danny recapped their story. As the teens made the police report, Shane pulled Chris aside. "Danny mentioned that you guys have seen some abnormal things in the woods around here lately?"

Chris crossed his beefy arms, the dark hair poking out of his rolled up flannel sleeves. "Yeah. At first we thought it was just a bunch of kids pulling pranks. Usually happens around this time of year anyway. But all of us, my wife included, have seen the lights. They don't look like flashlights." Chris glanced over at the cop and ran a hand over his mouth and bushy beard. He spoke quieter, prompting Shane, Emily, and Maria to lean closer. "We took a hunting party out one day earlier this month to see if we could find anything, but the guys got spooked. We couldn't see anyone, but every person said they heard whispers in different parts of the woods."

"And then Nathan Dass was murdered near the trail entrance," Shane added.

"Exactly," Chris said, stepping back. He gave his son a pointed look. "Which is why I want to know why my son thought it would be a good idea to go out solo to the woods with a few girls at midnight."

Danny spun around to the coffee machine again, busying himself with tidying the grains around the machine.

"Mr. Jones," Emily said. "How long has your family owned this place?"

"Three generations. My grandfather bought the land that surrounds here years ago to farm timber. He and my dad built the gas station in the forties."

She nodded, and Maria wondered where she was going with this. "And how many times have you been approached to sell it?"

He huffed out a laugh, "Hard to say. A lot of people have inquired about it over the years, but we'd never sell the gas station."

"But," Emily took a step closer, shrugging off her dad's hand at her elbow. "You're selling the rest of the land to the mayor?"

"How did you know that?" Chris said even as shook his head. He rolled the edge of his wiry beard between his thumb and forefinger as he spoke. "It isn't a done deal. We're still in negotiations but Clarissa keeps lowballing my dad. And it's contingent on her getting a rezoning permit, which everyone knows is an uphill battle in this town."

Emily and her dad shared a look. "There's something else." Emily added. "When we heard the whispers we started to look around the rocks to see if it was some other kid." She looked back at her dad, "We found a backpack instead. It was filled with candles, a bunch of spices, and a black salt rock."

The shorter blonde girl finally found her voice. "My mom said there's a cult here. That," she turned to Maria, "Sorry ma'am. They're saying the cult did something to Dave Fever's body to bring him back to life. And now he's stalking these woods."

Chris waved her off, but she persisted. "Everyone is saying it's the ghost of Dave Fever that killed that trucker. That even the Burial Rock Protector has left because of him. That's why no one has seen her this year."

Maria gripped the red string bracelet at her wrist, and everything else in her body seemed to seize beyond that string. She didn't believe in ghosts, but she also wasn't one to rule them out entirely if she saw one in person. It would be a cruel shift in fate if it was the ghost of Dave Fever that changed her mind.

"Enough, there is no cult, and Dave Fever's ghost is not lurking in the woods," Shane said. "Officer, can you get the girls home to their parents? Emily, Maria and I need to get home ourselves. It's almost two AM."

They piled into Maria's old Honda after a round of

goodbyes. "Dad?" Emily asked once the doors were shut.

"Not now, Emily. It's late. Let's get home so Maria can get some sleep at her own house."

He glanced over at Maria, his mouth a grim line. "You think you can pick me up in the morning? We can get my car and there are some things we ought to talk about. Might be a good idea for you to join me and my family for it."

She wondered at the seriousness in his tone, but it had been a whirlwind of a night between going to Greg's farm, her confession at Cate's, and now this. She nodded, and wove the car towards his dad's home under the bright moonlight. She was grateful for the officer stationed outside her house by the time she got back, but jumped at every shadow in her home.

There are no such things as ghosts, she told herself as she turned on every light in her bedroom to fall asleep. Her dreams devolved into nightmares of Dave's ghost watching her from the woods that night.

14

Raising & Raisin Toast

SHANE CRADLED THE LATTE Maria brought him in her car the following morning, trying and failing to not yawn in between sips of caffeine. The bags under his eyes were another level of terror, and no amount of cream would fix it. He let Emily sleep in, and filled his dad in on what occurred and what needed to happen next before he left.

He glanced over at Maria. She'd piled her riot of curls high on her head in a bun, and gestured with the hand that held her coffee as she spoke. She barely took a breath between words and he realized, albeit a bit late because of a lack of sleep, that she seemed nervous.

He put his hand briefly on her thigh to interrupt, "Maria, are you ok?"

Nervous laughter spilled out of her mouth as she gaped at him. "My dead husband, the one I murdered by the way, is apparently lurking in the woods around town." She shook her head, muttering something in Spanish before finishing, "So no. I'm not OK."

He smoothed down the stubble that seemed to point in every direction on his face, not quite ready to have the discussion he needed to have with Maria. He said instead, "Is that why you started wearing the Mal de Ojo bracelet?"

She held up the wrist tied with the red string. "This? No. Mama insisted we all wear one the other day. She's convinced that the rumor about the cult is true. I don't want to think about what she'll make us do if she hears it's Dave. And trust me… if Dave sucked that bad alive, I doubt death would have improved him."

Shane watched the road curve through the early morning fog. "The ghost of Dave Fever is not haunting this town."

"Of all the things I thought I'd need reassurance of…" She huffed out a laugh and took another long sip of her coffee, wincing at the heat. She jerked her head in his direction and asked, "Wanna tell me why you have a Mal de Ojo tattooed around your wrist?"

He thought back to the first of several botched attempts to Raise solo. He could still hear the ancient man's bones clicking around the room because he forgot the sumac. That sound, and the aggression rolling off the half decayed body from being disturbed, deterred him from trying again for almost a full year.

"I backpacked through Mexico after I left Hinnewatcha. I knew college wasn't for me, knew I wanted to get the hell out of a small town, but I had no clue what I wanted to do with my life. I'd gotten lost in a town called Tepoztlan, was flat broke, and wanted to get back to Mexico City. I'd made friends with a young woman who spoke English, and learned that her dad had died years before. She and her mother suspected the uncle, but couldn't be sure. I had a knack for figuring out problems, and gave it a go of solving the case."

Maria looked at him, dubious. "Solving a case in a foreign city where you don't know the language?"

She doesn't know the half of it. He thought back to the drunk night he decided he'd help. He later blamed the tequila for thinking it was a good idea to Raise a dead man in front of his still grieving daughter. Shane answered her, "I was arrogant. And dumb. But also had incredible dumb luck."

Fortunately his friend didn't call the cops when he took her out to the graveyard and dug up her dad's body. And she didn't have a heart attack when that body started to speak again.

"I was able to confirm their suspicions that it was the uncle, and they forced him out of the city. As a thank you, the mother tattooed the string on my wrist."

Por proteccion, she'd said.

"Anyway. That incident gave me the idea of what I could do with my life. I made my way back to Mexico City and flew straight to LA."

Maria pulled up behind his car and put hers in park. "Wait. It was that easy? You got a show on Bravo just like that?"

Shane laughed. "God no. I made these terrible business cards and tried my hand at being a detective for months. I thought I'd be a real Dick Tracy. I even wore a hat."

Maria laughed so he continued, grateful that the anxiety was out of her voice for a bit. "I happened to meet Frankie, my agent, by chance. I pitched him my services, and he said he had a better idea."

"He had that much faith in you?" She asked.

"Hell no. He didn't think I could solve anything. But I was a couple decades younger, had just spent eight months backpacking Mexico, and was still broke and barely eating. So I was tan, lean, and good looking. And he knew he could sell that."

"Least you proved him wrong."

Shane dropped his smile at that. "I don't think Frankie ever really thought I'd solve anything." He looked out the window as he continued, "Maria, there's a lot I need to explain, but you should know that my show... it's a bunch of B.S. Most of the time we already know who the murderer is, and I'm just there to confirm it. We usually research the hell out of a case beforehand." He ran his hand through his hair and added, "I'm totally out of my element here with Nathan Dass."

Maria looked puzzled, "But you figured out that I killed Dave? How'd you do that?"

"That's a longer story. I promise I'll explain everything when we get back to my dad's house."

She nodded, but didn't say anything else. He opened his door but she stopped him with her hand on his. Her eyes were on the rear view mirror, and as he turned, he saw a white SUV pull out of Greg Fever's drive down the road. Maria whipped around, squinting at the taillights as it sped off towards town.

"Do you recognize the car?" Shane asked, hopeful.

"I recognize the *I'd love to be your realtor* sticker. That was Clarissa Baker." She mimicked the mayor perfectly, "Town Mayor and Realtor Extraordinaire."

He filed that away. "I suppose that's not normal?"

Maria shook her head, "Nope. Clarissa wouldn't give someone like Greg Fever the time of day. Meet you at your dad's house?"

"Yep, I'll see you there." He stopped himself from leaning over to kiss her goodbye, startled at how normal that felt. He settled for an incredibly awkward fist bump.

***

Shane waited for Maria on his dad's front porch, pacing. She finished texting her mom that she'd be back after breakfast, and realized as she got out of the car that he was talking to himself. He met her as soon as she reached the first step, as if he didn't want her to go inside yet. Instead, he pulled her back down, away from the house and around the corner near the massive oak tree that reached high over the second floor. Its orange and red leaves matched the hue of the farmhouse it shaded.

"Maria," he said before pausing, as if to compose himself. "When we get inside we're going to talk about something that we have never told anyone outside of our direct family."

"Okay..." Maria replied. She'd had enough surprises in her life in the last seven days. The last thing she needed was for him to spring something awful on her. "Shane, should I be concerned?"

"No?" Shane said with a protracted shrug. He took her hands in his and led her to the swing under the thickest branch. "No, " he said more firmly. "It's not something bad. OK I'm doing this wrong. Here's the thing. It doesn't hurt anyone. It's something I learned from my mother, who learned it from her mother, and so on. And most importantly, I'm telling you because I trust you. And I don't want you to be scared."

"Full disclosure, Shane. I wasn't scared until that weird pep talk." She put her hands on both of his shoulders, "Just lay it on me. No more lead up."

He took a step back, swinging his arms back and forth as if readying himself. "Right. OK. Just straight out."

"Yep. Just say it."

He nodded, likely more to himself than her, and said, "I can raise dead people."

Not expecting that one, she thought.

Maria stilled, and a hundred thoughts fought their way to the front of her mind. "Maybe a little more?"

"Sorry. Right." He ruffled his hair so it stuck up at all angles before continuing. "When I was 17, my mother explained that our ancestors had a very bizarre, very rare, and very particular gift that manifested when we turned 17. Least that's how she prefaced it to me. She said we had the ability to commune with the dead. And we did it through a specific ritual that she taught me, that her mother taught her, and so on."

"Holy hell," Maria said. "You're dead serious."

He winced and nodded before gesturing to the old swing. "Maybe sit?"

"I think that's a great idea," she said, hitching her body up on the wooden seat. She held the ropes tight, welcoming their scratch as something concrete in a world that suddenly felt topsy turvy.

"I've never heard of anyone like us," he went on, pacing through the yellowing grass. "And again, no one, and I mean no one, can know about this." He opened his mouth as if to say something else, but seemed to decide against it.

"I can see why you wouldn't want anyone to know," Maria ventured. "So is this how you found out—" she trailed off, her mind racing ahead of her mouth. "Ohmygod. You're the cult! You're the one that messed with Dave's body? Like the salt and the herbs and stuff at the morgue?"

"Shhhhh..." He said, looking around like there would be anybody but his family here this far out of town. "Yes. That was me. And, well, Emily too, technically."

Maria's voice hitched higher, "You brought your kid to talk to a dead guy?"

"Yeah, well, I thought the more times she did it with me, the easier it would be for her later." Shane held up a hand when Maria opened her mouth. "My mom only showed me once. It took me a few tries before I got it right. And let me tell you," he huffed out a laugh, "it's not something you want to get wrong."

He had his hands in the air as if this were totally normal. He must have registered Maria's face because rushed to continue, "OK ignore that. But yes, I'm teaching Emily. Like an internship. An unpaid, very obscure internship that she can use as she sees fit, if she ever needs to, later on in life."

He ran his hands over his face, "I'm doing a shit job at explaining this, aren't I?"

"Sort of," Maria said, torn between the need to reassure him and the desire to wring every answer out of him. "So why did you bring me here to tell me? Why in front of your family?"

"I guess I thought it would be more believable if both my dad and my daughter could help me explain it," he said as he looked down. He'd never looked more vulnerable with her than in that moment.

Maria spun her grandmother's ring around her finger and watched him for a moment, deciding. "OK, Shane Bolles. Let's go talk about raising dead people over toast. Please just tell me there's more coffee inside?"

His long legs strode over to her instantly. He picked her up out of the swing as if she were a small child and not a woman grown. But she didn't stop him. Not when he grinned wider than she'd ever seen and hugged her hard enough to squish her lungs.

He pulled back and cradled her face in his hands. "Thank you, Maria Fever. Thank you for trusting me. For not freaking out. For listening." For a moment she thought he was going to kiss her, but he dropped his hands from her face and interlaced his long fingers through her right hand. "I promise, it won't make sense even after we explain it, but you'll believe me when I say Dave Fever isn't haunting Hinnewatcha's woods."

Maria smiled, and squeezed his hand once for good measure. "Good enough for me. Lead on, Dick Tracy. I'm going to need more coffee."

15

Stress Cooking

Shane led Maria into his dad's home and felt downright giddy. He never thought he would explain his gift to someone that wasn't family, and telling Maria was one of the most terrifying moments of his life. The fact that she hadn't run for the hills was enough to make him want to skip.

The smell of biscuits and grease hit them as soon as the door opened. He turned to Maria and warned her, "My dad is stress cooking. We're all a little out of our depth."

The kitchen had turned into a gourmand hoarder's paradise in the hour he and Maria were gone. Every surface held either a dirty bowl, a dish, or a tray full of pastries. Smoke billowed around his dad's large frame at the stove, and pans covered all four burners. Stacks of pancakes, sausages, and toast filled the countertops, and the table had enough juice varieties to rival a Vegas buffet.

Brandon Bolles shouted something to Emily in the other room, not hearing them enter.

"Dad!" Shane tried, but the man didn't respond, instead he continued to furiously stir eggs in a large blue bowl and leaned over to shift the pan of bacon.

Emily walked in from the other room holding plates and the cloth napkins his mother loved most. Shane let go of Maria's hand, not realizing until then that he still had it in a death grip, to meet her. Emily's wide, welcome smile at Maria chipped away at how mad he was at her for sneaking out the night before.

Brandon pivoted then from the stove, seeing them finally and almost spilled the bowl of scrambled eggs. His *Chunk of Hinnewatcha* apron had the C marked out with sharpie, and he rubbed his massive hands over it to clean some of the flour still stuck to them. Brandon gave Maria an all-tooth grin that only highlighted his nervousness, and told them to grab a plate.

Shane glanced over at Maria, wondering if this is when she'd bolt. But instead she took a plate from Emily and started asking animated questions to Brandon about what he'd prepared.

Emily hugged him. "I'm sorry again about last night. I didn't really think about the murder scene. I just wanted to find out if it was the Protector's voice that night."

"I get it. I'm curious too, but I don't think the dead are going to help us solve this one. But," he said, nodding in Maria's direction. "I did get more help." He ruffled her hair so she knew he wasn't as mad as he was the night before.

She glanced back at Maria, and Shane nodded his head. "I gave her the two-second elevator pitch outside. She knows."

"Dude!" Emily said, playfully shoving him out of the way to get a piece of banana bread. "You didn't even tell Mom, right?"

Shane ignored every piece of dieting advice he'd heard in LA and spooned the sausage gravy over his biscuit. "So?"

"Soooo," Emily continued, glancing again at Maria who was still peppering his dad with questions. "You told Maria. That's serious."

He rolled his eyes at her. "She needed to know. She thought, because of your little escapade last night by the way, that Dave Fever's ghost was haunting the town."

"Uh-huh. Right." Emily said, smirking.

"I'm serious!" Shane said, attempting to not blush in front of his 14-year-old. "Now shut up and give me that muffin."

After properly loading up, Shane grabbed the coffee pot off the burner and followed the other three into the dining room. Emily set the table with the white runner embroidered with lemons, the same one that matched the napkins. "My mom loved these," Shane told Emily, holding up a cloth napkin. "She had at least thirty different place settings, but the lemons were always saved for her favorite meals."

His dad caught Shane's eye and smiled. "And she never let us use anything but these ridiculous teacups with it." He held up the offensive sky blue china in between meaty fingers as if it were something alive and ready to run.

"Dad, I told you Maria was coming over maybe an hour ago. How on earth do you have this much food?"

"He has a freezer!" Emily interjected. "In the back. It's literally nothing but pastries and muffins. He came barreling up this morning before you even left the driveway and told me to pull out everything on the top shelves."

"I like having options," he sniffed. He nodded once in Maria's direction, "And it can't hurt to have something good to eat when we're having, uh, difficult discussions."

Maria chimed in merrily around a biscuit, "Like telling someone you guys are necromancers?"

His dad nearly choked on a scone, and Emily patted his back hard until he raised his hand for her to stop.

"The term 'necromancers' sounds a little dark," Shane said. "We prefer to call it a *Raising.*"

Brandon waved his fork in the air, "For the record, I am not one of them. I just married one."

"So, how does it work?" Maria asked, and Shane laughed when Emily shot her hand up in the air.

"Oooh let me, Dad! I've always wanted to try to explain this. And you were terrible when you told me."

"I don't think he's improved his explanation," Maria said, winking at Shane.

He sat back, smiling, and watched as Maria folded into their weird, bizarre life as if there was nothing more natural.

***

"So let me get this straight," Maria said after they'd gone round after round of her questions. "The spirit that shut Dave up mid-sentence—" she wagged her eyebrows at Shane. "That's my favorite part by the way. This spirit said there was going to be another murder here when we get a Moon Dog?"

"We're paraphrasing," Shane replied, topping off her coffee before refilling his own. "But yea, essentially. If you agree that the line '*Darkened moon meets the canine*' means a Moon Dog."

Maria shivered. Everything about this conversation made her want to grab one of her mother's rosaries off her wall. She asked, "When is the next Moon Dog supposed to happen?"

Shane leaned back in his chair. "That's just it. There isn't a specific day it's supposed to occur, but it's almost always just before a full moon wanes, which is two nights from now."

"On Halloween," Emily added. She stabbed another stack of pancakes and Maria wondered where she hid all the calories on her toothpick frame.

She gestured to Emily with her mug. "Remind me what Danny said again about the land sale?"

"He said Clarissa Baker had grown more aggressive about buying his family's land lately. She got mad at Danny's grandfather a few weeks ago because apparently she already spent a good chunk of money on plans and permitting fees. Said he verbally told her he approved the contract, and would sue him if he didn't sign."

"But why kill the trucker?" Maria asked, reaching for another banana nut muffin despite her jeans digging in her waist. "And other than us seeing her car at Greg Fever's farm today, what would tie the two of them together?"

Shane jumped up and hustled into the other room while Maria explained to Emily and Brandon that they'd seen her SUV pull out earlier that morning. When Shane came back, he pulled a small black box from his coat pocket that looked like a speaker. He pushed a button and heavy breathing sounds reverberated off the wallpapered walls. Emily's mouth dropped open.

"Ohmygod that's it! That's exactly what it sounded like at Burial Rock!"

He nodded at Maria. "I forgot to tell you about this until Emily mentioned the breathing sounds. I found this in Greg's RV just before I ran into you there."

"You did what?" Brandon asked, fist curling around his fork on the table.

Maria interjected before the father and son could start arguing again, which seemed to be a regular occurrence if the breakfast was any indication. "He helped me at Greg's farm. Had I not pushed him about accusing me of murdering Dave, he wouldn't have gone at all. If you get mad, get mad at me."

"I could never get mad at you," Brandon said, softening and patting her hand. He pointed back to Shane, "Now this idiot on the other hand—"

"OK, Dad, chill. We're fine. But we did figure out that Tat Face is staying on Greg's property."

"Wait! Don't say another word," Brandon said, pushing back from the table. "Emily, you clear off these plates. I'll get the whiteboard."

Shane reached over once the other two Bolles left the room. "You sure you're OK? I know this is a lot to take in."

Maria laughed. "That's certainly an understatement. But yes, surprisingly, I'm OK. It still makes zero sense and I think I'd die if I ever had to watch you Raise, but I'm fine." She refilled her water from the milkglass white pitcher on the table. "I'm just happy that Mama is taking Isa to Albany to see her sister for the weekend. I don't know how I'd be able to parent if I didn't have a little more time to digest all of this."

Regardless of the creepiness and unbelievable aspects of Shane's story, she was grateful. The prospect of a secret cult bringing Dave back to life was shaving years off her life. *Plus I'd never be able to get gas at Dan's Diesel again if Dave's ghost was lingering in the woods behind it.* Maria almost dropped her glass at the realization.

"Shane!" She said as Emily walked back in. "I know what Greg is doing with Clarissa. She hired him to set up those speakers around the woods, and now they're pushing the cult rumor ever since your fiasco with Dave's body. They're doing it to scare the Jones family into selling the land."

Emily nodded in agreement, "That would make sense why Greg would have the speakers hidden under his bed. He has nothing to gain by just scaring a bunch of teenagers."

"And," Shane added. "She's been talking about the cult to any and all of the wannabe sleuths in town. But why stage the backpack?" He turned to his daughter, "Did it really have all the same items?"

She nodded. "It looked like it. Red powder for the sumac, a black salt rock. All the same things we left at Memorial when Dave's Raising got hijacked."

"Greg told me the night of the first town hall meeting that he had an old girlfriend that worked at Memorial," Maria said. "She could have told him everything they found and he could have staged it at Burial Rock." Maria added, "Danny and his friends almost always camp there around

Halloween. Everyone knows that. Greg could have guessed he or someone in his family would see it. But I don't know how that links to Tat Face."

"Not yet at least. But we can find out from Chief Madison if they've figured out who he is," Shane said. "Maybe he really is just an old prison buddy looking for extra cash."

Emily rubbed her hands together and smiled. "So how are we going to confront Clarissa?"

"I could corner Greg?" Maria offered.

Shane shook his head. "Hard pass. He's too volatile, you've said so yourself. I am never putting you at risk. We'll find another way."

Maria's chest warmed at that, so she felt a smidge guilty about her Plan B. "I think I know a way to get it out of Clarissa then, but it'll require you to take her out on a date."

Brandon wheeled the whiteboard in the room then. "I found the other dry erase markers! What did I miss?"

16

Oysters & Babies

SHANE HELD THE PHONE out from his ear a few inches but could still hear Frankie shout.

"Two days?" Frankie said. "You dodged my calls and texts for two days! You do realize we're paying for a crew to be down there? Every day you don't appear on camera I'm losing money."

"Frankie, I get that you're mad—" Shane tried.

"Mad? No, I'm not mad. I'm *confused.* I gave you a homerun. Dave Fever fell in our laps and then Nathan Dass winds up murdered in the same picture-perfect fall town when you're already there less than two weeks later. It's the biggest opportunity for our show and you are throwing it away. Explain that to me."

Shane's stomach spun. He hated confrontation at all, and pushing back against Frankie when he was in this state was akin to doing a jig in front of a bull. "Frankie, I'm on it, but there are things you don't know. I took a GoPro up to

Dave's brother's property outside of town. We think he and the mayor are pushing these cult rumors to force someone to sell their land. We believe, and I'm working on getting the confession, that they killed Nathan Dass and are trying to pin it on the ghost of Dave Fever."

He smiled, *it's so ridiculous that it actually sounds like great TV.*

Frankie didn't sound as pleased as Shane. "Why didn't you show up to the appointment I made at the morgue for you to see Nathan Dass' body?"

Confused at the pivot Shane asked, "Why would I need to? I saw the raw footage Gary had from that morning and read the coroner's report. Throat slit. End of story. But anyway, I'll—"

Frankie interrupted, his voice low pitched and quiet, which was never a good sign. "Shane. I pitched this show. Me. *I* know what sells. And *I* know what isn't selling lately. The show has gone stale and we're losing viewers with every episode. So what I need *you* to do is to get on the goddamn camera and just go where I tell you. Got it?"

"No," Shane shot back. It was likely the first time Shane had ever said that word to him. Frankie was his agent, later a friend of sorts. They'd known each other for a decade and he was at almost all of Emily's birthday parties. But ever since Frankie invested in the show to become one of the producers, he'd morphed into someone else who felt like he could push Shane around.

Shane continued as Frankie took a large inhale on the other line, likely ready to shout obscenities. "No. I am not going to the morgue to film a ridiculous camera shot over a body bag when we know someone slit his throat. I'm going to solve this murder case. Then we'll film a documentary-style episode. And that's the shape of any future work I want to do together."

"Listen to me, moron," Frankie said. "You were a nobody before me, and without me, you're just some dumb blonde past his prime. Don't make me come there and—"

"And what?" Shane laughed. "Frankie, I may be blonde and getting old, but I know you. You're all bluster. You always have been. I'll get Gary and the crew lined up after I get this confession and then we'll let the viewers decide if I'm wrong."

"If you think—"

He hung up before Frankie could say anything more.

"Soooo, that sounded fun." Emily said, standing in the doorway. She joined him outside on the porch.

"Sorry kid. Thought you wouldn't be able to hear that conversation if I was out here," Shane replied. He sat next to her on the double swing and put an arm around her. "Frankie is all talk. And he's always mad. This is nothing new."

"Will he fire you?"

Shane shrugged, realizing then that he didn't care one way or the other. "He could cut the show. I'm sorry, I know how much that would bother you."

Emily laughed. There was a two-year span where she was mortified every time someone realized her dad had a reality TV show. She even refused to eat in restaurants in some parts of LA because he'd get recognized.

"I think you're doing a good job on Nathan Dass' case.

Even if it doesn't make it on TV, putting that atrocious mayor and her henchman behind bars is a good thing," she said.

Shane used his long legs to sway them and said, "Thanks, Buttercup. That means a lot to me." He kissed the top of her head. "What do you think of Hinnewatcha?"

"Honestly? I like it. I know I messed up sneaking out, but I really like Danny and his friends. They're genuine and not glued to their phones all the time. And, say what you want about small towns, but this one is obnoxiously cute."

Shane asked, "Would you want to live here?"

"Would you?" Emily countered.

"I think so. I'm tired of LA, Buttercup. I'm tired of acting. And of pretending. We could sell the house and pay all cash for something here. We'd have plenty leftover while I figure out another career." He couldn't deny that a particular local barista occupied his every other thought either.

She nodded. "I'm glad you said that. I'd love to live here. And the Old Man isn't so bad. Besides," she said, standing up. "I heard there might be a need for a new realtor in town. If you could sell some of the B.S. lines you did on your show, you can easily sell a house."

He mocked gaped and the pair of them laughed. She said from the doorway, "Chop, chop. If you're going to woo Clarissa into a fake date, you need to shower. You're looking rough."

Shane saluted her, and texted Maria on his way inside. *Meet me for a drink tonight?*

***

The cell phone ping forced Maria to pause her favorite garden therapy–ripping up weeds–long enough to read the text from Shane. She smiled, and gave another silent thanks for her mother getting Isa out of the house. *And thank you Tia Camila for getting Mama out as well.*

She thought through all the reasons why she shouldn't invite Shane over, but ended up telling him to come to her place later before all those nags in her head made her see reason. *It's not a date. It's just two friends having a glass of wine together.*

Maria felt lighter than she had in weeks, maybe years even. She didn't kid herself, she knew it was because the man that she'd dreaded seeing a week ago had somehow become someone she had to see again. He skipped through her mind, popping up in her thought process throughout the day. *I don't want him to fall in love with me. I just want him as a friend.* She began raking up the area where her new greenhouse would go. *Liar.*

Somehow in the span of a handful of conversations, she'd gone from seeing Shane as an adversary to believing he was the type of someone she wanted to wake up to. *No more falling for saviors, Maria. They always disappoint.*

She heard Levi Madison's voice before she saw him. He'd walked out the back of Cindy and Evelyn's home next door and joined the old couple on their patio. He was in plainclothes, and balanced a tray of oysters and grilling tools that he delivered to Cindy. She couldn't make out what he was saying, but he tipped his head back, laughing.

Evelyn waved hello and shouted over, "Maria! Come over! We're grilling oysters on the fire."

Her partner, Cindy, added over her shoulder, "Bring a glass with you. We're in a battle to see who will break down and do the dishes first, and I promise it won't be me!"

Maria chuckled and wiped the dirt off her jeans. She ducked inside just long enough to wash her hands and grab the plastic champagne flute from her windowsill that she kept for occasions just like this. Almost as soon as she stepped over the low fence, Evelyn embraced her, gripping her in her iconic bear hug: tight, warm, and long enough that Maria leaned into Evelyn's wiry gray hair. Their French bulldogs, Puddles and Pickles, ran circles around their feet, barking. Pickles wore a tutu today.

Levi nodded his hello as Cindy poured the champagne. Cindy & Evelyn were rarely seen without a bottle, and it was an unspoken rule that all champagne had a splash of OJ before noon and a splash of gin, lemon, and a sugar cube after dark. The sun hovered over the horizon, not quite ready to set, so it was just classic bubbles for their impromptu patio party.

The four toasted over the open fire. "What are we toasting to?" Maria asked, wondering again at how Levi seemed to be the couple's favorite Hinnewatchan after Isa.

"Halloween?" Eveyln suggested.

"Proper fall day?" Levi added, clearly at ease with the older couple.

Cindy looked pointedly at Maria and Levi and said, "To new beginnings."

Ahhh. Cindy is in matchmaker mode, Maria realized. She gave a tight smile, wondering how to diffuse the awkwardness threatening their toast.

Levi beat her to it. "Ignore her, Maria. Cindy and Evie have tried to play matchmaker with any single woman over the age of 18 and under 60 in this town. It was only a matter of time."

Cindy made a face at Levi, prompting Maria to laugh. Cindy clicked the tongs in Levi's direction. "Careful there, Chief. We're quickly running out of options so I may need to up that age ceiling. I heard the Book Club is looking for a new recruit, maybe I sign you up?"

"You wouldn't dare," Levi said. "Evie, please try to talk reason with your wife. I've told her a hundred times I'm not interested in dating right now." He looked over to Maria, "No offense, Maria."

"It's perfect. She's a window, you're a widower. You both live here and you're both attractive," Cindy said.

Evelyn laughed, "You mean 'widow and widower,' love. I don't think Maria is a pane of glass."

Cindy giggled and poured more champagne. "True. But you two would make great babies."

"There are no more babies coming out of me. I'm one and done," Maria said. She had no idea Levi was married before, let alone a widower. She wondered at what else she didn't know about the man.

Cindy pursed her lips, clearly shelving her efforts for a later time when Maria could be worn down. Evelyn pulled out their mismatched plates and the four of them hovered over the fire, eating oysters straight off the grill and chatting about Cindy and Evelyn's latest travels.

The oysters were all but polished off when they finally sat down in the rickety Adirondacks, Maria's hands sticky from the mignonette and butter. Evelyn reached over and patted her knee to ask, "Do you have a date set for the funeral?"

She didn't look at Levi, but felt his eyes on her nonetheless. "I haven't talked to Greg in a little while. He keeps wanting to push it."

Evelyn's sky blue eyes softened, and she asked, "But what do you want?"

Maria blew a curl that had come loose from her ponytail and answered honestly, "I want it to be done."

Cindy, louder than she was a few champagnes before, "Yea, but what's with all the rumors that someone messed with his body? Cate said someone had black salt and cilantro or rosemary all over him at the morgue."

Evelyn swatted Cindy to stop talking, and Maria glanced over. Levi watched her, assessing.

She thought back to the conversation she'd had with the Bolles that morning and tried to school her features. Her mother always claimed she looked like a fish when she lied, which just meant Maria had no idea what to do with her lips. She fanned herself, and pushed back from the fire that now felt too hot.

"I have no idea what that is," she lied.

When she said her goodbyes though a short while later, Levi said, "I'll walk you home. I need to bring you up to speed on a couple things."

She nodded, dreading whatever he needed to say that couldn't be said in front of Cindy and Evelyn.

"Maria," he said, once they'd walked to the far edge of Cindy and Evelyn's yard. "I didn't want this to get out, but

I found something disturbing that I was hoping you could shed some light on."

She had one leg over the low wooden fence and all but fell over at his statement. *Breathe, Maria. There are a lot of weird things going on in Hinnewatcha now.*

She ignored the hand he hovered out to her help over the fence. "OK. What is it?"

"Do you know if your late husband ever strayed?"

Maria laughed, her breath coalescing in the cooling October air. "Dave wasn't exactly the best husband, Levi. I never thought he was cheating, but I wouldn't put it past him. What did you find out?"

"Well, I don't want to badmouth a dead man," he started.

"He can't hear you," she replied, and then reminded herself she needed to lay off badmouthing him as well. The police didn't need to know she had ample reasons to want Dave gone.

Levi put his hands in his coat pockets, his stance wide as he faced her. "We got an anonymous tip from the county commissioner's office. Someone dropped off several printed pages of emails exchanged between the Mayor's office and among the board of commissioners. It appears that Clarissa Baker is aggressively pursuing a rezoning case for a property she is trying to purchase from the Jones family."

"Huh," Maria said, busying herself with picking off imaginary lint from her sweater.

Levi crossed his arms. "You don't seem surprised."

Maria blew out a breath. *I can't lie worth a damn, and we're going to need his help soon enough.* "So you know how I called the cops last night to meet us at Dan's Diesel?" She continued at his nod. "Shane's daughter told us a few things Danny Jones said that made us think Clarissa is bullying the family into selling their land for a lowball price. It wouldn't surprise me that she was using her weight as Mayor to steamroll the rezoning approval."

Levi didn't say anything, but used his usual long pauses to force the other person to say more.

It always worked on Maria.

She spoke in a rush, wincing at the freak out that would inevitably follow. "And, I might have gone to Greg Fever's farm to look around for those missing pills you mentioned."

He threw his hands up in the air. "Are you kidding me? Do you know how dangerous Greg Fever is when he feels cornered? Not to mention breaking and entering is illegal and I'm a cop."

"I know."

"Damnit, Maria. The same man you think is stalking you is living on Greg's farm. Did you know that?"

"Yeah we ran into him. Well, he didn't see us but we saw him when he came home and he almost caught us. Do you know who he is yet?"

He didn't hesitate. "Who is 'we'?"

Maria hoped her weak smile would calm him down. "Want to come inside for a cup of tea?"

"Not until you tell me what bonehead also thinks breaking and entering is a great idea," Levi said, scowling.

She rubbed her hands over her arms in the cooling temperatures and he caught the movement. He threw his hands back in the air and huffed, "OK fine. Inside. But no tea until we have this conversation."

He held open her back door that led to her tiny kitchen. She patted his shoulder as she walked in and said, "You're a good man, Levi Madison."

"Uh-huh. We'll see about that. Now out with it."

She relayed everything she and Shane learned, starting with the heavy breathing sounds in the woods, and the backpack of herbs and salt the kids found at Burial Rock, though she left out the Raising details for obvious reasons. She finished explaining how Shane got the speaker from under Greg's bed as the tea kettle whined.

Levi took everything in, unspeaking. He raised his eyebrows once but it happened so fast Maria couldn't be sure. He finally spoke. "Are you positive it was Clarissa Baker that left Greg's farm the next day?"

"Definitely. I saw her stupid sticker on the back of her SUV."

"You do realize that I can't use any of that in a search warrant? And I should charge you both with breaking and entering. I only told you about the pills so you would look in your *own* house. Not so you would go hunting for them at that psychopath's property in the middle of the woods." He pointed at her with his "I saw that" mug that depicted Jesus popping out at an angle. "No more sleuthing, Maria. Promise me you'll let us do the police work."

Someone knocked on the front door as it opened.

"Maria?" Shane called out. "I tried calling first, figured you might be out back."

"I'm in the kitchen—" she said, but he interrupted her before she could say anything else.

His back was turned to them as he shrugged off his coat. "Clarissa will be singing her confession this time tomorrow night. Tell me..." Shane trailed off as he turned and registered Levi's presence.

Levi crossed his arms and Maria winced again. "Shane, you probably ought to come in here."

"Oh. Hiya Chief Madison, I was just about to call you to discuss a few things my team has uncovered."

"Uh-huh. Maria, can you make a bit more tea? I have a feeling you guys are going to need it for the discussion we're about to have about law and order."

"Eh, might be time to switch back to wine," she said.

17

Date Night & Kidnappings

THE FIRE CRACKLED IN the hearth as Maria, Levi Madison, and Shane hashed out everything they'd discovered in her tiny living room.

"Levi, what made you ask me if Dave was having an affair?" Maria asked from her perch on the tattered red and white checked sofa.

As if Dave Fever wasn't already a piece of shit, Shane thought, wanting to murder the man anew.

Madison shifted in his spot by the couch, "In those emails I mentioned, the ones where Clarissa tried to force the board of commissioners into a rezoning? We found an email one of the commissioners sent a coworker about Clarissa's boyfriend, Dave, lurking around his office. They were afraid to go to the police because they assumed Clarissa would be notified."

Shane watched Maria for any hurt or indication that the news was painful. Instead, she just took a long sip of wine.

"Huh. Never thought Clarissa would date that low." She frayed the edge of the tasseled pillow in her lap. "In the last few months, Dave started going to his brother's place more frequently, like once or twice a week, when before he'd visit a couple times a month. It never occurred to me that he would be seeing someone else instead of just getting loaded on pills or beer at Greg's place."

"So you two never fought about Clarissa, or any other woman?"

Shane bristled. He knew where Levi was leading this inquisition, and any argument she acknowledged would give him cause to suspect she had a vendetta against Dave. But before he could intervene without being terribly obvious, Maria shrugged. "Nope."

She pivoted. "We still don't know why Tat Face is living at Greg's farm, though, right?"

He took a sip of his own wine to hide his smile. *Smart woman.*

She sat with her legs crossed under her, a glass of wine balancing on her knee. Her cream sweater nearly swallowed her whole, and she'd somehow tied her riot of curls up on top of her head with just a pen. Shane found it harder and harder to focus on the conversation each time a curl slipped loose and grazed her face. She was the opposite of the women he dated in LA. His ex and the few women who followed after her would try to look casual, but it never felt natural. As if everyone he'd dated tried to master the no-makeup look with Maria as their muse.

Chief Madison's gruff voice brought him back to the conversation at hand, "The guy doesn't even jaywalk, so we haven't been able to get his ID. His face doesn't show up on any database. Shirley even swiped a coffee mug he used at Cate's to run his fingerprints. Nothing. He's like a ghost."

"But he's still here? At Greg's farm?" Shane asked.

Levi nodded, "Yea. He occasionally goes to the grocery store or grabs a bite to eat in town, but it looks like he's settling in."

The trio fell silent for a moment. Shane couldn't tell Madison outright what the spirit warned when Dave's Raising fell apart, but he needed the cop to be on his toes. "Madison, tomorrow is Halloween. If Clarissa and Greg really are messing with dead bodies and murdering people in this town, tomorrow will be the best time for them to ramp up the rumor that Dave's spirit is haunting this place."

"I'm aware," Madison replied. "Clarissa sent out an emergency text to the entire town suggesting that trick-or-treating end by 6 p.m. It sent the local newsrooms into a frenzy. What time are you meeting her tomorrow?"

"One," Shane answered. "We're having a late lunch at The Flowering Wall."

Despite being the nicest restaurant in Hinnewatcha, The Flowering Wall still offered chicken fingers and fried mozzarella sticks. *Murderers can't be choosers,* Shane thought.

Once Shane told Clarissa that they may need her to be on the next take for *Dead Don't Lie,* Clarissa had jumped at the chance for lunch together. He didn't tell her that he intended to wear a mic for their prep session over lunch. Or that Madison and his team would now be waiting in the kitchen.

Madison stood up, shrugging his coat on. "I don't like

this plan. Mostly because it may get us nowhere, other than tipping off the Mayor that we know she's being shady. It's a giant leap to assume that she and Greg are murdering strangers just to scare one family."

"Thanks for the vote of confidence, Chief," Shane said.

"All I'm saying is don't get your hopes up. I have a laundry list of things I can't stand about Clarissa, but being stupid isn't one of them." Madison paused at Maria's front door, tapping the edge of the doorway, "And be careful. I'm keeping an officer outside until we have the perp behind bars and we're sure Tat Face is no threat."

"If he is here for good we're going to eventually have to rename him," Shane said. He surprised himself with how casually he referenced also staying here, and chided himself mentally.

Maria rolled her eyes and nodded to the detective. "Thank you, Levi. And I mean it, you're one of the good ones."

Madison gave a pointed look at both Maria and Shane, who wasn't about to get up to leave as well, but he didn't comment. He simply tipped his head once to Maria and walked out the door.

Shane waited until the detective was out of eyesight. "So... I noticed you didn't mention your plan about getting Greg fired up tomorrow?"

Maria gave a conspiratorial smile as she hopped up to refill their wine glasses. "What Levi doesn't know won't hurt him. And he'd never approve." Shane tracked her every movement, wanting to learn everything he could about this woman. He believed in life markers; events that demarcated everything before and everything after. Tonight felt different. The intensity between them built with every conversation, and being in her home, alone, with the fire and the wine was another level of torture. *Get it together. You're too close to dropping your bags at her feet and that's the last thing she needs.* He rubbed his hands over his eyes, blocking out the image of Maria for a moment while he got a grip.

She doled out a heavy pour before tucking her feet back under her across from him. "I don't want to talk about Clarissa or Greg or Dave anymore. Tell me something about yourself that no one else knows."

Shane laughed, grateful at the change in subject. "I'd argue that you know more secrets about me than anyone else."

"Nuh-uh," she said, waving her wine glass. "Raising the dead doesn't count. Your dad and Emily know that. I want something deep, Shane Bolles."

"Okay..." He set his glass down and leaned forward. He bit back a grin when she mimicked him. "But you have to swear you'll never tell another soul."

She held up three fingers, "Scout's honor."

"When I moved into LA, I couldn't afford much. I had to pick up odd jobs just to share a tiny bunk room with a few other broke kids downtown. One of my jobs was mopping the floors at this dance studio that rented space in the basement of our apartment building. It was a small place that mostly just catered to the film industry. Anyway, at the time, historical romances were gaining popularity and they were teaching actors how to do the quadrille, and the waltz, and the like for those British period pieces."

Maria stopped him, pursing her lips. "Wait. Is your big secret that you know how to waltz?"

"Oh, I know how to waltz, but that's not the secret, you impatient imp," Shane said, resisting the urge to drag her to him. "I would get there before my shift to watch the dancers and memorize the steps from the back. And when everyone left I'd try my hand at it in the mirror solo."

Maria cocked an eyebrow, waiting for the big reveal and gestured at him with her glass. "Let me guess," she said, clearly unimpressed. "You learned and that's how you bedded all the fabulous ladies of LA, by asking them to waltz?"

"No, actually the opposite. I learned, pretty well if I do say so myself, with a mop. But I never danced with anyone. Just that mop."

"Never?" Maria asked. "Not even at your wedding?"

"Not once. We eloped and Leslie thought the concept of the first dance was cliché." Then the best, or absolute worst, idea he'd ever had came to him. Shane stood up, unable to stop himself now even if he wanted to. "Maria, do you want to be my first dance?"

Maria's smile dropped, and she looked downright frightened for a moment at his outreached hand.

"I'm not going to bite you, " he said, laughing. "I just want to dance with you." *Please.*

"Here?"

Shane nodded. "Right now."

She didn't say anything for a beat, but then reluctantly put her hand in his. "OK... I'll do it."

He tipped his head back laughing at the dread in her

tone. He hadn't ever felt this much at ease with another soul, and for some reason, her disdain for dancing with him made him want to do it that much more. And it gave him the perfect excuse to hold her.

"There's no music," she deadpanned.

"Oooh. About that. Can't do music. I have to count," Shane said, a little embarrassed. "Just bear with me."

She softened at that, looking a touch less reluctant. He held his arms out and she placed her warm palm in one and the other at his shoulder. Her back straightened and before he even began she moved her first step back.

She blushed at his surprised face, saying, "I'm obsessed with Dancing with the Stars. I might have done a few solo waltzes myself."

Lighter than he'd felt before, he half led, half followed Maria around her living room, waltzing as they both said the counts aloud. They stepped faster with each turn around the room, and he held her a touch closer after every spin. Every time one of them stepped on the other, they'd burst out laughing. At one point, Shane miscalculated and hit her head against the side of the doorway. He might have embellished his ability to waltz, but she just grinned and leaned in for more.

Shane didn't want to stop, but he reluctantly did by the time they were both breathless. Her pen-held hair never stood a chance. He let go of her for a moment to release the remaining dark curls still intertwined around the pen. Maria stopped smiling, their faces inches apart. He didn't back up even though he knew he should. Instead, he ran his hands over her hair, righting it behind her shoulders and off her face as he'd been dying to do for hours.

***

Maria held her breath as Shane cupped the sides of her head, slowly running his hand down her hair and toying with the ends. *Shane Bolles is about to kiss me,* she thought, giddy and terrified at the same time. She hadn't been kissed in years. Dave was never the sort, and the last thing she wanted was his tongue in her mouth. *I don't know if I remember how to do this.*

He shifted forward and she tipped her head back, closing her eyes. But he muttered a curse under his breath. "I'm sorry, Maria. I can't do this."

Mortified, she stepped back. *Ohmygod you're an idiot, Maria.* She bit her lip, but it didn't stop the words from tumbling out. "Sorry! It's been a long time and I misjudged. I thought—"

He gripped her wrist, stopping her retreat. "No, you didn't think wrong. I'm sorry. It's me."

She shook her head, pointing at him. "I swear, Shane, if you give me the 'It's me, not you' line I will throw you out that window."

He ran his hands through his hair, mussing up its typical perfect style. "No. All I've been thinking about tonight is how I want to kiss you. But it's not fair, and it's not right, and it's not the time."

Maria warmed at his words. Or at the flush of wine in her system. Maybe both. She stepped back into his personal space. "It's not fair to who?"

"To you," he said, not making eye contact.

Bullshit.

She put her hands on his chest, trying to ignore the solid muscle under his crisp white shirt. "Shane, I consider you a friend. And friends don't B.S. each other. So explain why in the world a kiss would be unfair to me."

He didn't answer, but he didn't back up anymore either. He clenched his jaw and seemed to search her face, debating silently. "It isn't fair," he said, quiet and low. "Because you've been through hell and the last thing I want to do is put you in more danger."

"Danger? What are you talking about?"

He was silent long enough that she opened her mouth to push further, but he finally said, "There's someone back in LA that I'm afraid will hurt you to get to me."

Shane, who had been unnervingly cheery and confident at almost every turn since they'd met, seemed unsure of himself. Maria had no idea who would want to hurt him, but she realized that she didn't care who they were. Shane helped protect her from being thrown in jail. She would protect him, too.

She put both hands flat on his chest and toyed with a button. "Just tell me who this person is and we'll figure out the rest together."

He scanned her face, worry creasing his brows and angling his sharp cheekbones into hard lines. She reached up and ran her finger along the worry line between his eyes, trying to soothe whatever he was thinking. He closed his eyes and breathed in deep.

"Sit, and I'll explain," he said, resigned.

She took his hand, bringing him to the couch to sit next to her. The apple and cinnamon scented candle flickered on the mantle above the low fire, and leaves spiraled to the ground in a breeze outside the window. Only then did she notice that she hadn't let go of his hand, instead tracing the red Mal de Ojo tattoo along his wrist. He watched her fingers glide across the faded line and swallowed once before speaking.

"This past January, I was on a run a couple miles from my home. I had AirPods in, so I didn't see the van until it pulled up next to me. I wish I could tell you I fought back, or tried to run, but I was so startled, it didn't even register that I was being kidnapped until they threw me into the van."

This is so much worse than I expected, Maria thought, but kept running her finger along his knuckles as he spoke.

"Two men in hockey masks sat with me in the back, and a third man drove. That's all I saw before they put a bag over my head and tied my hands. I think I pleaded, bribed, and raged but they didn't say a word—not even to each other— the whole time." He watched her trace the back of his hands. "I think that was the worst part. The silence." Shane took another deep breath, and continued, "Anyway, I don't know how much time passed. It felt like hours and a thousand turns, but when they pulled the bag off my head I was in a dark warehouse."

"I could only see a few feet in front of me. They took me into a room with a single light bulb, and made me sit in a chair." He shivered and tipped his head back before continuing. Maria interlaced her fingers in his and he squeezed her hand before continuing. "The only person who spoke stuck to the shadows. I never saw his face. I could see silhouettes of other people behind him, one smoking a cigarette in the back. The main guy, the leader I guess, said they knew I had a gift with the dead. That I could speak with them."

"I tried to play dumb at first, but he didn't argue. He didn't say anything else at all actually. He just snapped his fingers and one of the masked men wheeled a dead guy out in front of me under the lights. Another brought a cell phone to me that had a live video feed of Emily at school. She was eating her lunch with a friend on the steps, laughing and had no idea someone was filming her."

Shane raked his hands through his hair again and Maria thought he might cry. She put her hands over her mouth, reminding herself that he was with her now. That he got out. That Emily was safe.

He leaned over, his arms resting on his knees, and watched the fire burn behind her. Maria ran her hands over his broad back, wishing she could take some of this pain away. She would have done anything those men asked if it were Isa.

He spoke again, quieter this time. "I didn't argue anymore. I just explained that I call it a Raising. That I was the only person I knew who could do it. And I listed off the things I would need and how much time we'd have with the dead guy. It turns out that he was killed by a rival gang. The leader just wanted me to confirm it."

"I'd hoped, like an idiot, that it would be done. They dropped me off at my home—they already knew where I lived—and just said they'd be in touch."

"And did they? Did they make you Raise again?"

He shook his head, "No. But they've called a few times, just to remind me that they'll require my services again soon, to not call the cops, et cetera. They asked how Emily was doing in her third period math class the last time they called."

Maria swiped a tear that threatened to fall before he saw. She doubted Shane, who was proud and confident at every turn, wanted to feel pitied. "When did you decide to leave town?"

"I came home late from filming one night. Emily beat me home. I pulled in and realized the van was parked outside of our home. I don't think I breathed until I ran in the house, but Emily was fine. Just asked why I was acting crazy. I called my dad and told him to expect us, and made Emily stay with a friend until we left the next day."

"Do they know that you're here?"

He nodded. "I tried to keep it quiet, but somehow word got out on the internet that I was heading for Hinnewatcha before I even left LA."

I did this, I killed Dave and brought him here. She put a hand on his arm, "Shane, I'm so sorry. If I hadn't killed Dave you wouldn't—"

He turned to her, covering her hand with his, "Stop, Maria. Don't ever apologize for killing Dave Fever. He was an atrocious excuse for a human being and deserved what he got. And I didn't come here initially for Dave, remember? I needed a place to lay low for a little while, and to see if they pursued me outside of LA. Dave's death just happened to occur before I got here. Besides, it only made national headlines once the trucker was killed. And the people that kidnapped me? They probably know where I am, regardless."

Maria stilled. "Shane, could Tat Face be here for you?"

He looked away. "I considered it. But I've never seen him on my own around town, only when I'm with you."

"We need to tell Levi. That cop doesn't need to be at my house. You need someone watching over you."

"Maria, there are two grown men living at my dad's house, and my dad can be absolutely terrifying when he wants to be. That cop stays at your house. I could never sleep if I thought you, Isa, or even your mother were in trouble."

Her slow descent into falling for this man became an abrupt fall into head-over-heels territory. She cleared her throat, trying and failing to focus on anything but how much she wanted to climb on top of him. "Have they called you since you've been here?"

He shook his head, "Not at all. But I still can't escape the feeling that something terrible would have happened if I hadn't left LA. Now I feel like I've dragged all this bad juju to our small town."

Maria chuckled. "Dave Fever was an awful person long before you came back, and Clarissa and Greg have apparently been terrifying the kindest family in Hinnewatcha for months. This place is cute, but it's far from perfect. You didn't bring this here, so don't add it to the list of things to worry about. Sounds like you have enough."

Shane smiled so wide his dimple showed, the same dimple Maria had definitely not been drooling over in every one of his episodes. He bumped against her shoulder, pulling her hand back in his to rest on his knee. "I'm sure they're going to reach out at some point. But for now, I think I'd rather take my chances here." He was quiet for a few moments, his eyes on the fire.

Then he tipped her head so could look her in the eyes, his thumb brushing the side of her jaw. "Do you understand, though, why I don't want anyone to know you're important to me?"

Her pounding heart all but stopped at his words. She nodded, unable to form sentences just yet. She swallowed once, and then dramatically looked over her shoulders, "But I don't see anyone here, do you?"

He laughed and wrapped his hand around her thigh, pulling her closer to him so their legs were flush on the couch. Maria leaned into him, lining her body against his side and propping her chin on his shoulder. She said quietly, "No one will know, Shane, if you kiss me tonight."

He watched her in that intense way that made her toes curl. He slowly shifted them so they faced each other directly again and tucked a curl behind her ear with his other hand. "When I finally do get to kiss you, I don't think I'll ever stop. Not in public, not in private. And I will want the world to know that you are mine, and I am yours, Maria Fever."

"Oh," was all she could say at first. "That's a really good answer. You should have led with that."

Shane laughed, and though the tension between them was still palpable, she understood. She added, "I filed for the name change yesterday. It's back to Maria Cruz now."

"That sounds so much better," Shane said, bringing her

hand to his lips and kissing them lightly. Once, twice. He sighed and started to stand up, "I should go."

Maria didn't let him up. "You should…But Isa isn't here. Neither is Mama. I won't throw myself on you, yet," she added, and he laughed. "But you should stay here tonight."

He shook his head, "You do realize this will be absolute torture for me, right?" His smile grew and his eyes narrowed on her.

She bit her lip, grinning back. "I think you can handle it."

He ran his hand over his face and for a moment she thought he'd kiss her, their conversation be damned. He scanned her face, unspeaking, and she held her breath. She resisted the urge to whoop in victory when he finally nodded. "OK. I need to text Emily, though. I'm never going to hear the end of this."

18

Mozzarella Stick Take Down

Shane fiddled with the mic under his collar again while he waited at the table. Chief Madison's team waited out of sight in the kitchen. All of his focus should be on the lunch date he was about to have with Clarissa Baker, but his mind kept drifting back to the previous night.

He'd woken up in a tangle of Maria's curls on the couch with her sprawled over him, dead asleep. She didn't wake up, even when he threw a blanket over them and held her in the early morning light. He was exhausted from staying up late and fighting his baser urges that he didn't see Clarissa until she reached his table.

She leaned over him for a hug, and he half stood, half crouched in an awkward embrace. "I'm a hugger," she said. "And you looked lost in a daydream. Hope it was fun?"

"Sorry, not much sleep last night," Shane said, stretching his neck to make sure the mic hadn't dislodged in the hug.

"Tell me about it. I can barely keep up with all the projects

I'm juggling. I can't imagine how hard you must be working to stay looking that fit and manage your TV empire. Have you ever been here? I just love this place. The chicken piccata is to die for—"

Clarissa rambled on, her bright white teeth flashing with every other word. With matte red lips, she looked every bit the former beauty queen. Her blonde waves and Botox brows barely shifted as she spoke animatedly about everything, and she waved or pointed to almost everyone in the room to mouth hello throughout her unending monologue.

"Oh, I'm ready, are you?" Clarissa said as the waitress reached them. "I'll have the strawberry salad please, but no strawberries and I'd rather have pine nuts instead of pecans. And maybe arugula instead of spinach. What kind of cheese do you have?"

Shane stifled a groan and glanced down at his watch as the poor college kid listed off the various cheeses in the kitchen. Maria would be texting Greg just after 12:30, which, according to Cate, was when he ate lunch in town most days. Shane needed to get this conversation moving before Greg showed up.

"Do you want to be naughty?"

He choked on his water, "Come again?"

Clarissa smirked across the table and did a little shimmy in her seat. "Yes, let's do the mozzarella sticks, too, to start." She winked at him and stage-whispered behind her hand, "They're my favorite."

"So," she said, drumming her coffin-shaped nails on the table as soon as the waitress left. "Tell me what you need from me, Shane. I'm an open book."

"Perfect," Shane said, leaning forward so his best angle was aimed at her. "I'd like us to talk through what my team has discovered so we can determine if there is anything of value you can add to this upcoming episode." He had a feeling that she'd talk more if she thought she needed to prove something. "But, what I really want to discuss is an opportunity for a new TV show. You see, I've always loved my hometown, and I think there is enough interest in Hinnewatcha now to pitch a show to HGTV about new families moving here."

She put her hands flat on the table, "Stop it. I have *always* thought the same thing. I don't know if you know this, but I'm the top realtor in this area and I know this place like no one else."

"There's one issue I see though," Shane said, leaning back. "There just isn't that much available real estate, you know? It's like people move here and never want to leave."

"Exactly! I've been saying this for years. It's like you and I are on the same wavelength. Just not enough inventory."

"Right. And, I don't know real estate like you do, obviously," Shane said.

Clarissa smirked and swatted his hand on the table. "Stop it. You're going to make me blush."

Not with that much bronzer, Shane thought. "Well, it's true. Anyway, when I drive around I see so much land just outside of town. And I keep wondering, why aren't there any neighborhoods here?"

Clarissa's eyes lit up. "Yes! Like why so many trees? I think the same thing. And I'm glad you mentioned that," she said as she leaned down to her luggage-sized purse. She pulled out a heavy binder and oriented it to Shane on the table. He ran his hands over the slick compilation of stock photos of kids on bikes, families grilling, and a white picket fence community.

Clarissa leaned forward and drummed her lacquered nails over the binder cover. She dropped her voice lower and looked around before continuing, "I'm going to let you in on a secret before anyone else. I'm working on this planned community development that would be *perfect* for the show and we're just about to break ground."

Shane flipped through the pages, pausing his skim every now and then as if he gave a damn. "Wow, this is—this is something else. It looks amazing. Where is it?"

"You know the trails behind the gas station where Burial Rock is?" She took a bite of a mozzarella stick and continued, "That's about a hundred acres, and will easily accommodate this first phase of development."

"Huh," Shane said, leaning back. "I thought that one old guy owned it? Dan Jones from Dan's Diesel? I didn't know he sold."

She stopped chewing for a moment, "Well, he *is* selling. There are some minor paperwork things, titles, boring stuff you don't care about, you know, that I'm working through. But it's as good as done."

"So you aren't actually about to break ground then?" Shane asked as nonchalantly as he could, "What's the timing?"

"Shovels are ready, Shane, don't you worry your pretty little head," Clarissa said, smiling wide. She held her fingers in the air to mimic a pinch. "There's just this one teensy, little, *tiny,* thing that needs to happen, and then we're full force."

"That sounds great," Shane lied. "And the rezoning? That's all finalized?"

Come on, Maria. Need Greg here.

"Look at you, Mr. I-don't-know-much-about-real-estate," Clarissa said, reaching over to pat his arm. She lingered on his bicep, squeezing once. "Believe me, it's as good as done. The thing about being mayor is that you have access to some extra, let's just say, *levers,* to pull when you need them."

Shane glanced down at his watch again and tried not to smile as he asked, "Like access to Memorial's morgue after hours?"

***

Maria wiped down the same clean spot again on Mama Cate's counter, thinking through all that could be happening at the restaurant around the corner. She tipped her head to Emily across from her. "OK, walk me through this again? I don't want Greg to have your phone number."

Brandon Bolles spoke just as Emily opened her mouth. "It's an app. We found it on TokTik, it masks your phone number."

"Pops. For the last time, it's called TikTok," Emily said, rolling her eyes. "Anyway. The Old Man is right. I can text Greg through the app, and a different number will show up on his end."

"Got it, " Maria said, holding her hand out. "Let me read it one more time before you send it?"

She took the bejeweled iPhone from Emily and walked around the barista counter, away from Cate and the handful of customers. She read aloud, "*Looks like your partner in crime is spilling your crimes to the TV detective at The Flowering Wall. Do you want to comment?*" She looked up from the phone, "Wait, who is ScrappyRoo?"

"It's my alias," Emily answered as she wiped off the whip cream stash from her hot chocolate.

"I like it. And the photo of Clarissa talking to your dad is perfect, nice touch." Maria handed back the phone. "Let's do it."

Emily cracked her knuckles while Brandon paced behind her, chewing on his nails. He checked his phone less than a minute later. "Cate just texted from the diner, said Greg just picked up his phone."

The diner was at the opposite end of the block, at the furthest end of Main Street. If Greg took the bait, he'd walk right by Mama Cate's. Maria wrung the rag over and over in her hands as they watched the windows.

"This is too much," Brandon said, hopping a little in his space by the counter. "What if he doesn't go?"

"Relax, Pops. You'll give yourself a hernia. Even if Greg doesn't confront Clarissa right now, Dad might get a confession out of her on his own. I don't know why, but Dad has this way about him that makes people want to tell him all their secrets."

"Don't I know it," Maria muttered, her eyes never leaving the window.

Greg Fever didn't walk by.

He ran.

The three of them high-fived each other, and a few minutes later Cate walked in.

She pointed a finger at the trio. "I don't know what all that was about, but I know I don't like being kept out of the loop. Now spill. What are you three up to?"

Maria replied, "I promise, Cate, I'll tell you everything later. It'll be worth the wait."

Her boss harrumphed as she picked up a package that a customer dropped off. "Oh, I meant to tell you. You know Nathan Dass?"

Brandon leaned over the counter. "The trucker that was murdered? What about him?"

"Craziest thing," Cate said, closing up the box with screeching packaging tape. "Nina, our late night shift barista, said he delivered a package here just before he was— you know—" she slashed her hand across her throat, miming the murder with a click of her tongue. "And the foolish girl didn't think to tell me until this morning."

"So?" Emily said, but Maria was a step ahead of her.

"You opened the package, didn't you?" Maria said as she eyed the pile of packages waiting for pickup.

Cate shrugged, "Obviously." She leaned over her package to point at them with the roller of packing tape. "But get this... the box was empty."

"Why would Nathan Dass deliver an empty box?" Brandon asked.

Maria stilled. "Cate, who was the package addressed to?"

Cate shelved the box on the pallet for the FedEx pick up and said over her shoulder. "Ivan Melnyk."

"Who?" Maria, Brandon, and Emily asked simultaneously.

Cate mock gaped at them. "The guy with the face tattoos? He only orders flat whites whenever he comes in? I thought I told you that. His name is Ivan Melnyk. Anyhoo, he hasn't come in here in a few days and the package was pushed off in the corner because of the crowds. I don't have a number either, so we'll just wait and see when he picks up his empty box."

Maria walked over to the shelf where they kept delivered packages, skimming the names. Emily and Brandon peered over her shoulder as she set a medium-sized box that was light as a feather on the counter.

"To Ivan Melnyk, c/o Mama Cate's," Brandon read aloud. Maria pointed to the return address, and he said, "From Ivan Melnyk? But that's an LA address. Why would he send an empty box to himself?"

Emily pulled Maria and Brandon back a few steps, whispering out of Cate's earshot. "Face Tat, Ivan, I mean, must have confronted the truck driver when the box was empty. Maybe the trucker took something? Drugs?"

Brandon shook his head, "Cate said he hasn't been in to get the package. How would he have known it was empty, if he has yet to get the package?"

"Because he mailed an empty box to himself." Maria rang the rag out in her hands again, twisting it over until it was taut, as she mused aloud, "He mailed it via a special carrier, Freight Folks. He must have known Nathan Dass would deliver it somehow."

"We need to tell Dad," Emily said as she turned to leave.

"This means Clarissa and Greg didn't murder Nathan Dass."

Maria stopped her, "No. You stay here. We all promised Shane we would not go in there because Greg is too much of a loose cannon. But the cops are in there now, your dad will be safe. I'll text Levi and we'll tell Shane as soon as we see him."

***

Clarissa spilled the sip of water she was about to take, "Sorry, what did you say?"

Shane looked over Clarissa's shoulder to see someone running this way from the opposite side of the block.

Bingo.

He leaned closer. "Look, I get it. Sometimes people just need a little push in the right direction. I think the stuff Greg Fever did to his brother's body is a little creepy, but brilliant. That had to be you, right?"

"I don't know what you're talking about," Clarissa said, her smile slipping to a thin red line.

Shane scooted over so he sat in the chair next to her, instead of across. He spoke low and leaned in. "The whole rumor? The one that said a cult brought Dave Fever's spirit back and he's haunting the woods outside of town? I just assumed that was you so you could scare the Joneses into selling. Greg Fever is an idiot, he couldn't have thought that up on his own."

"First, I don't associate with Greg Fever's type, if you get my drift. And I definitely didn't give him access to a dead body. And I—"

He interrupted her, "But you were at his farm? My

cameraman saw you leaving the other morning." *No need to say it was he and Maria that saw her.*

Clarissa looked around her before hissing, "Are you following me?"

Shane gave a protracted shrug, the one that Emily always claimed was his tell. "Me? No. But I just assumed that it was you hiding the speakers in the woods. The ones meant to scare the Jones family? That was a great idea."

Clarissa leaned in close, her Miss Vermont smile long gone from her face. "You listen to me. I don't know what you're talking about, but we're done here. You'll be hearing from my attorney."

She jumped as the front door banged open behind her, startling her and everyone else in the restaurant. Greg Fever pointed a finger at Clarissa, "You two-timing bitch! I knew you'd cave."

Clarissa stammered, "I'm s-sorry..have we met?" Her face turned red as she met the eyes of all the curious patrons..

"Don't even try that." Greg loomed over Shane, "What did she tell you?"

"I haven't said any—" Clarissa tried, but Shane interrupted her, again.

"She said enough, but what I want to know is how much she paid you to kill Nathan Dass. Surely, she didn't have the nerve to slit his throat herself?"

Greg's eyes grew wide and he shook his head as Clarissa started to protest in earnest. "Hell no. I didn't kill anyone! Is that what you told him?"

"Greg, stop talking," she said, pulling out her phone.

"Nope. No way. I know how this plays out. You get to

keep your hands clean and you put me behind bars, so I can't get my cut." He shook his head in disbelief, clenching and unclenching his hands. "You said I murdered someone?"

"She was going to cut you in after you murdered the trucker, right?" Shane asked, holding his hand up just enough so Madison's team didn't interrupt, yet.

"I didn't murder anyone! She paid me and Dave a little cash to scare the Joneses. Everyone knows that old man thinks ghosts are real. All we did was hide speakers in the woods a few times with these scary noises, so they'd get freaked out enough to sell. That's it!"

"What about steamrolling the commissioners? Was that you or her?"

Clarissa stood, facing Greg, phone to her ear. "Stop talking, he's riling you up. I've got my attorney—"

"Bullshit. If we're getting the record straight I'm gonna make sure everyone knows it wasn't just me." Greg pointed a finger at Clarissa and stood in her way when she made for the front door. "She and Dave were bumping uglies. Said she needed him to follow around the head commissioner, to spook him, you know? She said she'd cut us into the development deal if we got the Jones family off the land and the commissioners to agree to the new zoning. That's what got Dave murdered. I think he knew too much so she had him killed."

An officer was pushing back the small crowd forming outside of the restaurant, but neither Clarissa nor Greg paid them any attention.

"Oh please. That's ridiculous," Clarissa hissed, phone forgotten. "You're the moron that apparently got caught on camera at the morgue messing with Dave's body. You're the only one that stood to make any more money if Dave was out of the picture. Did you kill your own brother for more of a cut?"

"Hell no, he was the only family I had left! I would never kill him." Greg seethed. "And I didn't do any of that to his body in the morgue. It was your idea to set up the backpack in the woods with all the same stuff and push that rumor." Greg turned to Shane, "Dave came to me before he died and said Clarissa was all mad because he wasn't scaring the commissioners enough. Wanted him to rough one up a bit. I told him to stop sleeping with her. I didn't trust her, but Dave said I was being paranoid."

Clarissa huffed, "He's lying and none of this will hold up in court. Now get out of my way!"

Greg put his hand on the door, shutting it as she tried to pry it open. Someone at the table behind her held their phone up, filming. "I have a recording to prove it," Greg said. "I made Dave take one the last time he met with you. I took it out of his pocket the night I found his dead body." He looked at Shane, "Dave was at her house just before he got killed and the tape has the two of them talking about roughing up the commissioner. What do you think of that, Mayor?"

Detective Madison and his deputies came out of the kitchen, guns up, startling Greg back to the wall. "I think we got enough, Shane, don't you?"

Clarissa snarled at Chief Madison, "If you even think of putting me in handcuffs, I'll have you fired." She tossed her perfect highlighted waves over her shoulder. "I'm the goddamn mayor for crying out loud. My attorneys will eat you for lunch."

Cameras were snapping outside as Shirley led Clarissa Baker outside in handcuffs, despite her threats. Greg put his hands together in front of him. "I don't care. Take me. I didn't do anything. Everyone knows the Joneses don't care if you camp near Burial Rock. Everyone does it. Trespassing won't hold up."

"What about your new roommate, the guy with the face tattoos? Did he kill the trucker?" Shane asked as a deputy clicked the handcuffs over Greg's wrists.

"What?" Greg said, stopping in the doorway before the other officer could escort him out. "Wait, you think he killed the trucker? That guy just came into town and said he was looking for a place to live. I got nothing to do with him." Greg held his handcuffed hands up even as he was pushed out toward the waiting cop car. He said over his shoulder, "I don't even know the guy's name. He had a stack of cash. Said he'd pay me double if I didn't ask any questions or mention him to nobody. I didn't give a shit what he did, but I didn't tell him that. I gotta eat, you know? Nothing illegal about that."

Madison stopped at Shane's side as Clarissa and Greg were put into two separate cop cars. Shane crossed his arms and looked at the police chief. "What do you think?"

"Not sure, but I'll take that wire from you and let you know." Madison nodded his head in the direction of the departing police cars. "We have Clarissa on intimidation at least, but that recording device from Greg would help if it's true. He's right about his part, though. Trespassing won't hold up, since the Joneses have always let the public hike those trails." Madison shrugged, "We may get him on an accomplice charge."

"Neither of them confessed to Nathan Dass' murder," Shane acknowledged.

"But we have a name now for Tat Face. Ivan Melnyk. Somehow Maria discovered it and texted me while you were talking to Clarissa. I'll put Shirley back on him after we book those two clowns and we'll see why he's hanging around here." Madison took a deep breath and blew it out, shaking his head. "Even if he didn't murder the trucker, he's hiding something."

Shane unhooked his wire and gave it to the detective. "I'll touch base with you in a little bit." He glanced down at his phone, skimming through the onslaught of text message alerts he'd missed in the last hour. "Shoot. I gotta go, my cameraman is freaking out about something."

19

Bagging It

Maria paced the Bolles' kitchen and looked out the window again, trying to ignore the merry-go-round of panicked thoughts traversing her mind.

"It's getting dark, where would he be?" Emily asked. She looked smaller than ever as she burrowed further into one of her dad's hoodies at the kitchen island.

Brandon whipped the frosting in the plastic bowl he had in a death grip. "Cate said she thought she saw him get in the *Dead Don't Lie* van when she walked down to talk to The Flowering Wall owner. He's probably still filming." He put the bowl down and pulled out a spatula to decorate another dozen stress-induced cupcakes. "Maria, read me his text again?"

She pulled her phone from her cardigan and reread Shane's text from hours before, though by now she could recite it word for word. "*All went well. Clarissa and Greg in jail. Still no answer on who killed Nathan Dass. Call soon, need to do a little work.*"

"Emily," She asked, "If he went to film a scene with his cameraman, how long would he be gone?"

Her freckles were pale against her skin under the white farmhouse light above her. "A few hours? Maybe? But it's almost six o'clock."

Maria smiled tightly, trying not to scare Shane's daughter. Her mother had texted photos of Isa and her cousins dressed up for Halloween earlier. If Maria went missing, the last thing she would want is for someone to scare Isa. *He's not missing Maria, he's just working late.*

And yet, as much as she tried to reason with herself, something felt off.

"I'm sure he'll be here soon," she lied. "I'm going to step outside for some fresh air." She walked out the back door, past the whiteboard with the Bolles' sleuthing notes taped up. A stick figure with face tattoos now had "Ivan Melnyk" under it. Despite their best attempts, the internet had nothing on him.

The Bolles' farmland stretched out in neat rows behind the house, disappearing around a low hill in the distance. Night settled quickly this time of year, and she wished she was with Isa trick-or-treating, not worried about murders and murderers. She tried to focus on the cool air going in her lungs to calm her nerves.

It didn't work.

She dialed Levi only to get his voicemail again. The wind picked up, pushing the only wisps of clouds past the moon. She froze.

Two lights, like eyes, were on either side of the moon.

Screw this.

She ran back inside, "Brandon! There's a Moon Dog. I'm going down to the station to get Levi. Emily, call Shane's agent, Frankie? See if he can get in touch with the cameraman."

Before either Bolles could say anything, she darted to her car. She sped out of the driveway and began a mental list of all the places Shane could be, and everything they'd discussed about his kidnapping. There weren't that many places in town that could be used to hide someone. Her chokehold on the steering wheel tightened when she remembered how he'd gripped her hand last night.

He must have been terrified when that bag came off his head in an abandoned warehouse.

Her thoughts turned to Nathan Dass and what they'd found out about him, as she flew around the curves leading back to town. *It keeps coming back to Tat Face. And now LA.*

She double-parked her car in the station's parking lot as Levi walked out, cell phone in hand.

He met her at the car, "I was just about to call you. Sorry, we've been at it for hours with Clarissa Baker's attorneys. What's wrong?"

"Shane hasn't come home, yet," she said. "Is Shirley still tailing Ivan Melnyk?"

He opened the police station door for her to walk ahead of him. "She left for his place right after we booked Clarissa and Greg. Problem is, he never came back to Greg's property. We've got an alert out for his car, but I'm spread thin because of all the trick-or-treaters and news vans."

Maria tied her curls up on top of her head. "Do you

have a map? There are a few places I think he might have taken Shane, but we'll need to narrow it down."

"Whoa, back up," Levi said. "Why would Shane be in trouble?"

She couldn't explain all of his story, but Shane needed her, and she needed help. "He was kidnapped in LA by some gang earlier this year. They put a bag over his head and took him to a warehouse. They keep threatening him."

Levi stood feet shoulder width apart and held his hand up so she couldn't walk further. "And neither of you thought to mention that?"

"I'm sorry, he didn't tell me until last night. I don't think he wanted to tell anyone."

"What did they want?"

Maria couldn't very well tell him that Shane raises the dead, so she just embellished a little, "To extort him, money I think? Something about his show. And when you were arresting Clarissa and Greg, we found out that Nathan Dass was in town to deliver a package for Ivan Melnyk. It was an empty box from Ivan, to himself from a P.O. box in LA. I think Melnyk is part of the gang that kidnapped him."

The muscles in Levi's cheek went taut as he unclipped a radio on his belt. "I need a high alert on Ivan Melnyk's car," he said into the radio. "This takes priority; consider him armed and dangerous."

He gestured for Maria to walk again, "Come on, I have a map in my office. Show me where you think he is."

***

Shane worried at the ropes that bound his hands behind

his back, trying anything to loosen them. He could hear his cameraman, Gary's labored breathing somewhere to his left.

It felt like hours since he got into the news van only to find a masked man holding a gun to Gary's head. The kidnapper didn't say anything. He just handed Shane a cell phone with a map pulled up. Shane took one look around at all the wannabe sleuths and reporters in the town square and nodded. He navigated for Gary and when they finally stopped, he knew what to expect.

Just do what they want. They need you, and once you're done, you and Gary can both go home.

The bag finally came off his head, and he blinked in the dimly lit storage unit.

Frankie stood at the far end, smoking a cigarette.

"Frankie?" Shane asked, his feet thrashing against their restraints in the metal chair. Even as he spoke though, all the pieces started to fall together. "What are you doing?"

"I told you," Frankie said, stomping on his stump of a cigarette and pulling out another in one fluid move. "I needed this show to make money."

The man behind Shane took off his ski mask, and Shane jerked back at Frankie. He blurted, "You're working with Tat Face?"

"I needed you to Raise Nathan Dass," Frankie ignored his question and walked closer. The rancid secondhand smoke hit Shane harder each time Frankie gestured with it. "I lined everything up. All you needed to do was go to the morgue, do your thing, and I would have caught it all on camera. We'd be rich, Shane. You just needed to do this one little part and we'd be rolling in it. Do you know how much we would have made with one YouTube video?"

Shane needed to keep him talking, which would be easy because he had a thousand questions and Frankie loved to talk. Madison was planning to tail Ivan Melnyk again. They would eventually find him. The rope cut further into his wrists as he balled his fists behind him. "When did you find out?" Shane began. "And how?" Gary turned toward him and Frankie with each question, as if he watched a tennis match under the brown bag covering his head.

"The Milkman Murder. You were always so cagey and private about the morgue visits. Something seemed off. I thought you might get your kicks rubbing up on dead bodies or something, so one day I beat you to the morgue and hid in a closet." He ran a manicured thumb over his hairy knuckles, each one cracking as he spoke. "I wanted to see what was going on. And lemme tell you—I almost shit myself when I saw what you were doing."

Shane felt like an idiot. He had taken so many risks, and had grown so comfortable with the Raisings over the years. He should have known that Frankie would have followed him one day. He should have realized why he kept pushing to show the bodies on the show. He fought back the nausea threatening to overtake him.

"So you're the one that killed the trucker, Nathan Dass, then?"

"I didn't," Frankie said, pointing to himself, and then at Tat Face. "But he did." He took a seat in the empty chair across from Shane. "Don't get worked up about that piece of crap. Nathan Dass was almost $80K in debt with Ivan's boss. He was going to die one way or another." He took another drag on his cigarette as his gold bracelet slipped down into the sleeve of his Dolce and Gabbana silk shirt. "He needed to die; I needed a body. It was a win-win so more people wouldn't get hurt."

Shane breathed through his mouth. His stomach was already doing flips and the musty smell of the empty storage unit and the too-familiar Marlboro Light smoke made his stomach roil. "You were there when I was kidnapped before. That was you in the back of the warehouse smoking, wasn't it?"

"Yea, but trust me. I didn't wanna be." He glanced over Shane's shoulder at Tat Face standing guard. "I didn't have any choice in the matter. I owed his boss a chunk of cash. I got over my skis in LA, and I needed an influx of cash fast."

Shane deadpanned, "Glad to hear you decided to sell me out to fund your bad habits."

"Look," Frankie said, pointing the cigarette in Shane's face. "I invested everything into your show because I knew one day your little special powers would get out and I'd have it all on film. But the Brigazis called in their advance before I could catch you on camera. I had to tell them what you could do. It's not my fault they wanted to see it in person."

"Nothing is ever your fault, right?" Shane said, laughing. "I'm responsible for your new boats, all the women you chased, and the private planes you took everywhere. You can do math, Frankie. At some point it was going to catch up to you."

"Don't get high and mighty on me, Shane. I watched you whore yourself through LA and I know what it's like to keep up. I'm the one that thought of DDL. I *made* you. And all I got was a joke of a percentage for signing you with those producers that tanked the show. None of this would have happened if our viewership hadn't taken a nosedive."

"You. Are. A. Producer now, Frankie." Shane said, shrugging his shoulders. "If you're so much smarter than us and so much better at show business, why weren't you able to turn the show around?"

Frankie smiled and leaned forward over the folding table between them. "What do you think I'm doing now?" He held his hands out wide, gesturing around the stuffy, dark room. "I'm turning the show around."

Shane's stomach dropped with the sickening realization of why Gary was bagged next to him. He strained against the ropes, "Frankie. Don't do this. We'll figure out another way."

"Wish I could. But I'm out of time and out of options." Frankie rubbed his hand over his stubble and glanced down at his phone. He looked past Shane's stricken face to Tat Face, "We have enough viewers now. It's time."

Tat Face moved behind him, and Shane recoiled while asking, "Time for what?" He dreaded the answer but needed to keep Frankie talking.

"Can't have anyone saying we green screened this," Frankie said as he set up a tripod in front of Gary's chair. "We're live streaming in four minutes."

Gary's muffled cries started anew as he shook his bagged head back and forth. Shane shut his eyes against the onslaught of light as Tat Face turned on the yellow work lights staged around the storage unit. Each pop of a bulb made Gary flinch, and Shane racked his brain for every threat he could say to slow this down.

"I won't do it. Live stream all you want. You'll be caught on camera killing someone, they'll triangulate your location, and I'll just sit here until you're arrested or you kill me, too. But you can't make me Raise someone."

Frankie threw a small duffle bag on the table, thudding in the hum of the lights. "I got everything you need in here. Sumac, the salt, white sage. It's all here," he said, ignoring Shane's threats. But Shane clocked the way Frankie's hands were shaking, even if his voice sounded calm.

Shane's metal chair screeched loud over the concrete floors as he strained against his ropes. "I'm serious Frankie! I won't do it. You'll kill him for nothing."

"No," Frankie said, sweat beading on his bald head. "We killed Nathan Dass for nothing. Ivan here had the cameras staged and everything, but you refused to go see his body. Gary's death will be on you, and this time, there's no backing out."

Shane shook his head in disbelief. "How delusional are you? Didn't you hear me? I said I won't Raise him. Go ahead, kill him," he silently apologized to Gary in his head, and hoped Frankie wouldn't call his bluff. "I don't care about him. I won't Raise him."

Frankie kicked the chair across from Shane and pointed to Tat Face as the chair clanged against the metal wall. "Do you know who they wanted to kill? Emily was at the top of the list. Then they pivoted to your dad, thinking you'd cooperate better if they could use the threat of hurting Emily to entice you. Ivan suggested we grab your new lover on the way here, but we couldn't because a cop car was parked outside of her house."

"It won't end, Frankie," Shane said, blocking out the images Frankie had conjured. "Don't you get that? Even if you think you can get out of this with your hands clean, they'll be able to tell anyone that you were an accomplice. Where do you think you're going to go?"

"China? Vietnam? Saudi Arabia? I can think of a lot of nice places where a man with money can live large that don't extradite to the US." Frankie stood behind the camera across from Gary and said to Ivan, "One minute."

Ivan pulled his ski mask back over his face and stood behind Gary. He pulled out a serrated knife and Shane started to pray silently in his head. Frankie wouldn't kill Shane if he knew he could make money off of him, but Gary was a loyal friend. He didn't deserve this. Shane struggled with the ropes to no avail. He had never felt more useless as Frankie counted down from 10 aloud. Gary must have caught on because he wept under his hood, the sound echoing as Frankie silently mouthed the numbers once he hit three. Frankie's three fat fingers shook even as he leaned down to view the camera angle.

Gravel sprayed outside the storage unit, pelting against the metal like gunfire. Frankie tumbled back in shock, tripping and knocking over his tripod and camera as the roll-up door was thrown open. Red and blue lights filled the space as Chief Madison and four other police cars waited on the other side, guns drawn.

"Hands in the air!" Madison shouted.

The sound of the knife clattering to the concrete was the

best thing Shane had ever heard. He took deep, gulping breaths, not caring that tears rolled down in his face. He sunk back against the chair, his bones loose, grateful for being tied down still. He didn't think he'd be able to stand just yet. An officer took the bag off Gary's head, and his mottled red cheeks shook as he screamed his rage at Frankie.

"I will kill you for this. I know people in every prison, Frankie. I will make your life hell. My cousins will drain the life from you even if I don't."

"It was a s-stunt!" Frankie said, cowering in the corner and backing away from the officers approaching. He held up his hands, placating. "It just went too far, ask them. Shane, tell them I would never do something like this. Tell them. You know me. It was just for show."

Shane rubbed the feeling back into his wrists as the cut ropes fell. "I don't know anything Frankie. I'm just a dumb blonde past his prime, remember?"

"Maria, stay in the—" Madison tried, but Maria was faster. She ran to Shane, knocking him back against the chair as she embraced him.

She ran her hands up and down his sides and face, searching for injury. "Are you hurt? Bleeding?"

He wrapped his arms around her, squeezing tight and inhaling the melon scent of her shampoo. The adrenaline was draining from his body, and with each exhale he melted closer to her. He held her flush against him as Tat-Face-Ivan and Frankie were read their Miranda rights. "It's ok. I'm ok. It's ok," he repeated, though if he was trying to reassure her or himself, he couldn't be positive.

Gary, in all his sweat and cigarette scented glory wrapped

his arms around both of them. "Thank you Shane." He wet kissed both of Shane's cheeks before he could stop him. "I'll bury him for both of us."

"Easy, killer," Shane laughed, clapping him on the back." Prison is punishment enough. I don't think it's dawned on Frankie that his weekly pedicure won't happen in jail."

Frankie struggled against the officers, leaning back as far as he could to face Shane. "Shane, call our attorney. I can't do prison. I'm not made for it. It was just show business. Stop pushing, just give me a minute."

He switched tactics. "I'll tell everyone what you can do. How you solve all the cases. You owe me, Shane Bolles. I'm going to get what I'm owed."

Maria's hand tightened in his as Gary stepped between Frankie and them. "Every prison, Frankie. I know someone in every prison. Not great for family reunions, but it sure does come in handy to have as many shady relatives as I do. You say a word about Shane, and I'll make sure they find you."

Frankie, for once in his life, appeared lost for words as the officer shut him inside the police car. Shane asked, "You going to be OK, Gary? Do you want to stay with us at my dad's house?"

He ran his hand over his bald head, "Thanks, Shane, but I think I'm going to head to my mom's house in Queens." He smiled at Maria as he patted his pockets for his cigarettes. "No offense, but I think I've seen as much of this town as I ever want to."

Gary followed an officer out the door as Madison

clapped Shane on the back. "Want to tell me what that was all about?"

Shane flushed, "Ah, money? Frankie got upside down with a gang back in LA. That bled over to me."

Madison didn't blink. He just waited. "Uh-huh. And the rest? You want to explain what it is that your producer thinks you do to solve cases?"

Maria shouldered her way in front to stand between them, but Shane spoke before she could fire up a defense. "I don't think you'd ever believe me, but I can promise you this. I'm done solving cases." He pulled Maria flush against him, his chin on her shoulder. "Besides, you look to be doing a pretty good job without any of my involvement. Thank you."

Madison just shook his head. "Thank Maria, had she not come to us when she did, we would have been too late."

"I have every intention of thanking her thoroughly once we are alone," Shane grunted as Maria's elbow found his stomach.

"Fine. We'll recap in the morning. You two go home," Madison said, hugging Maria briefly and then turning to the other officers.

Shane and Maria climbed in the back of another cop car, his hand never leaving hers, as they called a relieved Emily and Brandon. They sat flush against each other in the back, the energy between them intensifying as he tried to follow the officer's small talk. All he wanted now was to get Maria alone and have her hair fan out around them as he ran through every dirty thought he'd ever had about her. He palmed her thigh, pulling her closer. His thumb ran over the inseam of her jeans and he smiled when he realized she was gripping the edge of the seat. When the officer reached his dad's gravel drive, he couldn't wait any longer. He blurted, "This is good, officer. Thank you. We'll walk the rest of the way."

Maria cocked her head as he pulled her to the shed at the edge of the property a few yards from the mailbox. "Where are we going, Shane? Emily and Brandon will be waiting for us. They're probably on the porch already."

He pushed her against the back of the old wooden shed, pinning his arms on either side of her head and lined his body up close to hers. "That's exactly why I needed to get you to the shed. It blocks the view and I don't think I can take another moment without kissing you."

She didn't have time to respond as he cradled her head in his hands and finally, *finally,* kissed her. It was thorough and demanding, and an absolute tease because the more he kissed her the more he needed to kiss her. She gasped when he picked her up to get a better angle, and she wrapped her legs around his waist, alternatively digging her nails into his shoulders and back and gripping his hair.

She broke the kiss as he moved to her neck, "Shane. Your family is frantic, we have to go."

"Uh-huh, we need to go." It took a few more minutes though before he could pull himself away from her lips, and he reluctantly let her slide down his body to touch the ground. "OK. Give me a minute."

Maria looked flushed, her lips puffy under the full moon from their kiss as she tried to right her riot of curls he'd mangled. When he felt in control of his mind again, he pulled her to him to walk down the long gravel drive.

"What now, Shane Bolles? Back to LA?" Maria asked as she kept her gaze ahead of her.

He bumped her shoulder with his, and kissed her hand intertwined with his own. "I have zero intention of moving back to LA, Maria. You are my home now. In fact, I have no intention of being away from you for more than the few hours necessary each day for us to make a living."

She smiled wide, turning to him. "Oh is that right? And do I get a choice? What if I don't want to date you?"

"Well then, you're just going to have to kill me," Shane said, grinning.

She punched his arm, "That's not even remotely funny." But she barked out the laugh he wanted to hear again and again as his dad's porch light came into view.

20

42,000 Pumpkin Spice Lattes Later

ONE MONTH LATER, HEAT crept up Maria's cheeks as she tried, and failed, to ignore the Book Club meeting on the other side of the barista counter.

Shane held court in the tattered leather chair by the fireplace. Attendance was higher than ever at today's meeting, and the circle of old women leaned in close around him in their chairs. He held a paperback book in one hand, its black and white cover a close up of a shirtless, muscled man. Shane's voice rang out dramatically, "—felt like a rocket, huge and hot, vibrating on the launching—"

I'm going to die, Maria thought, putting her hands over her ears. A moment later, victory was sealed amid the cackling. The women of Hinnewatcha chanted, "Shane! Shane! Shane!"

He propped one long leg up on the table next to him amid the shouting and clapping and took off his belt. He swung it over his head, smiling broadly as if he'd won an Emmy. Cate was shimmying with the belt around her hips in the background as he sauntered over to Maria a minute later and kissed her soundly.

Maria laughed as the gleeful shouts grew louder behind them. She and Shane waved them off, arms around each other as they walked out and onto Main Street.

"I suppose congratulations are in order?" Maria said as she righted the scarecrow outside of Mama Cate's.

Shane brushed back his hair, and said, arrogant as ever, "Puh-lease. I was a shoe-in. I could have read the back of an Imodium box to those old horndogs and still won."

Maria shoved him, but he caught her hand and brought it to his lips. "No, I am not talking about the Book Club," she said, grinning. "I'm saying congratulations because Mama just texted. You're officially under contract for the house!"

Shane whooped and swung Maria around before kissing her again. Her mother pounced on the lack of realtors in town and got licensed in record time. She brow beat the old pharmacist into selling his home to Shane the same day she became an official realtor. Turns out Rosa Cruz' intimidation skills came in handy.

They crossed the gas lit lamp square, slowly making their way to Maria's home a few blocks further. Painted pumpkins with cursive sayings like "Give Thanks," and cornucopias sat on each front porch they passed. Maria sighed, "I will miss your dad's daily breakfast buffet though."

"Eh, his stress-baking will be coming to a close soon enough," Shane replied as he interlaced their fingers together again. "The LA County office called to say the Brigazi gang is in a bloody turf war. Ivan's boss and the three other men that kidnapped me were killed."

"Wow, never thought I'd be happy to hear about that much violence," Maria said. "What did Levi say about Ivan's extradition?"

"He'll be transferred out of the US within the next few weeks. And we'll have Frankie's court date pretty soon."

Maria's mind flashed back to the moment she saw Shane bound in the storage shed. If she'd been seconds later, things would have been so much worse. She squeezed his hand in hers, reminding herself that he was ok. They still had the threat of Frankie telling someone else about Shane's ability, but his cameraman assured him that he would keep Frankie quiet. Turns out, Gary really did have an alarming number of familial connections in jails throughout California. And he reminded Frankie of that fact at every trial.

Levi was waiting for them on Maria's front porch, a manila folder in his hand. Despite the friendship they'd made in the hectic weeks leading up to Frankie's arrest, Maria's stomach always dropped when she saw him. Shane pulled her closer, lessening some of the unease with his steady presence and ever-cheerful attitude.

He gave his best *Dead Don't Lie* smile and shook Levi's hand, and the two chatted about Shane's departure from his Bravo TV show. Maria glanced over to see her neighbors, Evelyn and Cindy, sitting on their front porch with the two Frenchies dressed up in sweaters. They turned away quickly at Maria's look. Too quickly, in fact. Panic started to claw its way up her throat. To distract herself, she wrapped her arms around Shane's hard waist and reminded herself she wasn't alone now.

"So I'll get to it," Levi said, turning his attention to Maria. "It turns out that the analyst working Dave Fever's case made a mistake in his toxicology report." Levi glanced once to her neighbors and hit the manila folder in his hand against his leg. "I owe you an apology for the back and forth. It looks like Dave did die of an overdose."

Maria leaned on Shane, so she didn't fall over as Levi continued, "—and Greg has asked for special permission from the courts to be released to scatter his ashes all along his farm. Do you have any objections?"

Maria could have hugged Levi, and schooled her features so he didn't question the grin threatening to break her cheeks. "No, I think that sounds peaceful. Dave would have liked that."

Levi said his goodbyes and Shane and Maria slowly walked into her home. When the bright yellow door was shut they both did a shimmy in her foyer. She jumped into his arms for another kiss. It would have gone on longer had they not heard the chorus of gagging noises in the kitchen.

"Cut it out!" Isa shouted.

Emily added, "Aren't you guys sick of that yet?"

They laughed and walked in the kitchen only to freeze again. The kitchen counters were covered in small photos of Shane in his signature *DDL* pose. He grinned at them from buttons, posters, and flyers with red, white, and blue backgrounds.

"What are you doing?" Maria asked, picking up a poster that said *Vote Shane Bolles.*

Shane read aloud, "Hinnewatcha Mayor? Really Emily?"

She shrugged. "I found a job where your cheesy lines

might come in handy. Besides, you're unemployed. Chop, chop!"

He laughed and turned to Maria, "You think I stand a chance?"

She leaned into him and pinned a button on his shirt, lingering there for a moment. "Oh I think so. But we need to start with the Book Club ladies. They might have some ideas for a better photo."

The End.

Acknowledgements

To my readers, thank you so much for picking up this book! I'd love your help spreading the word about this story, and the best way to do that is to write an Amazon or Goodreads review. I'm terrible at social media, but I promise to update my profile with news of more books, so please follow along at ccyork.writes.

To my editor and alpha-reader, Amy Carden, I'd be completely, endlessly, and a thousand more adverbs lost without your advice. Thank you for all your insights, questions, and polite suggestions. I swear one day I'll write a paragraph without an adverb before your first read through. Next book. Your talent for storytelling and writing is top notch, and I'll be the first to buy *A Pentacle of Witches*.

Mallory Muetzel, thank you for the book and writer nerd convos, for your beta reads, and for inspiring me to finish this book faster than I thought possible. I can't wait to see *The Favored Vessels* published!

To my parents, Lynn Stotz and Dan Stotz, thank you so much for your unwavering support and love for my family.

Em, your stories continue to be my all-time favorite. I want to see *The Cozy Detective and the Fancy Bandits* on shelves one day. Batey, you sat down next to me a moment ago and asked who you should marry. I think you have time since you're only five, but I appreciate the fact that you're already a romantic at heart. I love you both.

D, you make this life awesome, worthwhile, exciting, and comforting. I love you. I promise not every book I write will have a spouse killed off.